Morgan slowly rose from his seat. "Excuse me." His brows snapped together, and he came out from around his desk.

Kathleen stood defiantly in front of him. "You asked me out, then, what...changed your mind or got a better offer?"

Morgan was confused, but by the scowl on Kathleen's face he knew she believed what she was saying.

"And another thing, mister." She used her right index finger and poked him in the chest. "You don't say all those beautiful things to a woman and just kick her to the curb without an explanation."

Morgan grabbed her finger and held it at his heart. "I didn't kick you to the curb, and I certainly didn't blow you off. You said you were leaving early and doing something with your sister this weekend. I'd say you blew me off."

"No, I didn't." Kathleen stepped forward, closing the gap between them.

Morgan watched Kathleen's face morph from anger to confusion to desire. He could see how sincere she was, and he was overwhelmed with emotions. Morgan lowered his head and gently kissed her on the lips. Kathleen slid her hands up and around his neck, pressed her body against him and moaned his name into his mouth. Morgan deepened the kiss.

Dear Reader,

If you have read any of my books, you know how important it is that my stories come from a place of love, based in some truths, and showcase strong and sometimes unique family dynamics. I hope The Kingsleys of Texas hasn't disappointed. So far, you have met three amazing men. Now it's time to meet the final Texas Kingsley.

In *The Heiress's Secret Romance*, Kathleen Winston is a special agent for OSHA determined to bring down the Kingsleys for perceived malfeasance against their employees. Morgan Kingsley, the second eldest of the Kingsley brothers and a proud commitmentphobe, finds himself second-guessing his thoughts on the subject after spending time with Kathleen.

I love interacting with my readers. Please let me know how you liked Morgan and Kathleen's story. You can contact me on Facebook or Twitter, @kennersonbooks. I hope to bring you more exciting stories of fascinating families shortly.

Until then,

Martha

the HEIRESS'S SECRET *Romance*

MARTHA KENNERSON

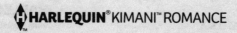

HARLEQUIN® KIMANI™ ROMANCE

Recycling programs
for this product may
not exist in your area.

ISBN-13: 978-1-335-21684-7

The Heiress's Secret Romance

Printed in U.S.A.

Martha Kennerson's love of reading and writing is a significant part of who she is, and she uses both to create the kinds of stories that touch your heart. Martha lives with her family in League City, Texas, and believes her current blessings are only matched by the struggle it took to achieve such happiness. To find out more about Martha and her journey, check out her website at www.marthakennerson.com.

Books by Martha Kennerson

Harlequin Kimani Romance

Protecting the Heiress
Seducing the Heiress
Tempting the Heiress
Always My Baby
An Unexpected Holiday Gift
Be My Forever Bride
The Heiress's Secret Romance

Visit the Author Profile page
at Harlequin.com for more titles.

I'd like to dedicate this story to all my faithful readers. If not for you I would have all these stories and characters stuck in my head with nowhere to go. Thank you for your continued support.

Acknowledgments

I would like to acknowledge all the survivors of Hurricane Harvey. Houston showed the world just how resilient we are.

Chapter 1

Kathleen Winston walked into her office, still in shock at how badly her meeting with her boss had gone. Twenty-nine-year-old Kathleen was an heiress to the multibillion-dollar Winston Construction fortune, but still worked as a special agent for the Occupational Safety and Health Administration. She released a string of profanity under her breath, dropping down into her chair. Kathleen turned away from the desk and looked over at the framed picture of her parents sitting on the credenza. Memories of the day her parents had sat their children down to explain their mother's illness were very vivid. It was also the day that changed the trajectory of her life.

Hearing her mother say the words *I have cancer* had been a knife piercing Kathleen's heart. She still felt as if the conversation had just taken place versus seven years earlier. Initially, Kathleen thought her parents were playing a very bad joke. At least she hoped they were. After all, their mother showed no signs of being sick. She was still strong, energetic and very beautiful.

But Kathleen quickly realized how serious things were by the pained look in her father's eyes.

Don't worry, Mom. I'll get them, just like I have all the others.

"What's wrong?" a voice from behind asked.

"Everything," she replied, immediately recognizing the speaker. "Simpson just killed my investigation into Kingsley Oil and Gas."

"And you're surprised? Girl, you know you can't trust no Simpson," Gilbert replied, laughing as he approached her desk.

Gilbert Ray was Kathleen's assistant and best friend since they were kids. He was one of two people at her office, the only one besides her boss, who knew her background and wealth.

"What did he do now?"

Kathleen turned and faced Gilbert. She smiled at the baby-blue suit and white dress shirt he'd paired with a blue-and-white bowtie and blue-and-white loafers. Kathleen loved the fearlessness of her friend. He always knew who he was and he never cared about what others thought about him.

"My…my, don't you look fabulous."

"Don't I?" He glanced down at himself. "I love that green Michael Kors camouflage dress you're rocking too."

"Thanks."

"Dish—what happened at the meeting?"

"Just what I said—Simpson pulled the investigation into the Kingsleys and their company," she explained.

Gilbert gave a nonchalant wave before he took a seat in one of the round chairs that sat in front of her desk. "Girl, I don't know why you are tripping. You know how you beautiful, rich, bougie people do stuff like that. If you want something to go away—" he used his hands to imitate making a phone call "—like on that game show, you use a lifeline and call a friend."

Kathleen sighed. She knew Gilbert was still upset about the way his wealthy boyfriend of nearly a year had recently ended their relationship. Kathleen sat up in her chair. "First, I know you're still salty about what Vince did, and I hate that he made me tell you what an ass he'd been, but I couldn't have you thinking something happened to him when he stopped returning your phone calls."

Gilbert smacked his lips. "I know, and I love you for it."

"Good. And I love you too. Second, I told you to stop calling me that and don't lump me in with all bougie rich people."

"But you are…both. Rich and high-class and you know it too." He frowned.

"I'm a melting pot of things, and I embrace them all," she stated matter-of-factly.

"Okay, Miss Thing. You beautiful, long haired, high-cheekbone-having, sophisticated, successful, thick-lipped melting pot you," he teased. "You're certainly rich, though."

"Excuse me, Miss Winston. Mr. Ray, the postman just dropped off the mail."

Gilbert looked over his shoulder. "You see that tray on my desk with the sign that reads Mail Here? Why don't you drop it right there?" he asked sarcastically.

"Oh… Okay." The young lady turned and hurried off.

"Thank you," Kathleen yelled after her. Her eyes bored into Gilbert. "Really?"

"What?"

"Why are you so rude to that young lady?"

Gilbert shrugged. "She's an intern."

"And you're acting like a mean girl. Stop it. It's not a good look."

"Fine." Gilbert rose from his seat. "I'll go buy the child a cookie or something. Speaking of buying things, when are you going to give me one of those black cards of yours and let me buy you some better chairs? Something nicer than these fake leather things you're forcing your guests to endure. Better still, a whole new office set for us both."

"This is a government office. We have to accept the furniture they already provided us. So deal with it."

"At least you get to fix your office up with a few antique knickknacks and those beautiful and costly contemporary artworks that grace these ugly walls while I'm stuck out there in a world full of gray."

"Oh please, talk about knickknacks. Your colorful accessorized cubicle brightens up the whole floor," Kathleen complimented him, smiling.

"True. I do love all the colors in my rainbow flag."

Kathleen laughed. "That you do."

"What were we talking about?" He tapped his index finger against his temple. "Oh yeah, the fact that you're rich and still hiding it."

"No, we were talking about what Simpson did, and my father's rich," she corrected.

"So what do you call that mega trust fund you got when you turned twenty-five or what you'll get at thirty?"

"My father's legacy…not mine," Kathleen stated expressionlessly. Her cell phone rang, and she looked at the screen. "Speaking of which…"

"You talk to him. I'm going to make a coffee run. Will you be having your usual?"

"Yes, thanks." Kathleen answered her phone. "Hi, Dad."

"Hello, Kathleen. How's my beautiful daughter?" he asked in his native French.

"I'm fine, Dad. How are you?" she replied in English. The phone fell silent, but she could hear background noises, so she knew what had happened. Kathleen repeated her statement and question, only this time in French.

Kathleen's Creole father was from the North American island of Sint Maarten. Along with her mother, the product of a Caucasian and Afro Caribbean relationship, he raised their children to speak both French and English. However, her father preferred that they converse using his native language.

"I just want to confirm that I'll be picking you up tonight at your sister's place."

"We talked about this, Dad. I have a lot going on at work and I really can't afford to—"

"What? Take a little time out to celebrate your mother's legacy and help raise money and awareness for her foundation's mission?"

"That's not fair, Dad. Of course the work of our foundation is important. But so is my job. I'm helping to ensure others don't have to go through what we did."

"And I'm proud of you for it too. Yet you have a responsibility to your family as well," he reminded.

Kathleen sighed. "Well, it looks like my workload has just lightened a bit, so yes, Dad, I'll be there."

"Good. Make sure your sister is on time. You know how she can be and I hate being late," he stated, his voice firm.

"Yes, Dad. We know. We'll both be ready when you get there." Kathleen heard her boss's voice before he appeared at her door. "Dad, I have to go. Love you, and I'll see you later."

Simpson stood in the door with his hands in his pockets. "The French language is beautiful."

"Yes, it is," she agreed.

"You didn't have to end your call on my account," he stated as he entered the office.

"Are you all right, Mr. Simpson?" Kathleen frowned. His gray suit was a bit wrinkled; he could use a haircut and he looked like he needed a nap.

"I haven't been getting much sleep, and I'm not feeling well."

"Maybe you should go see a doctor," Kathleen suggested.

"I'm on my way now, but I wanted to tell you that I think you're right."

"About the Kingsleys?" Her eyebrows snapped to attention.

"Even though all the allegations of wrongdoing by the Kingsleys and their company have been proven false, and Evan Perez, the man behind the false narratives, is behind bars, this most recent accusation didn't appear to come from anyone Perez hired. I still can't believe he thought he could get away with trying to ruin the Kingsleys, who were basically defending themselves from his many attacks. He was the one who started their war in the first place," Simpson offered, shaking his head and taking a seat.

"No, it did not. Mr. Silva seems credible and is not a part of some big conspiracy," Kathleen stated with conviction. "His only concern is about the safety of his fellow employees and ensuring their company has competent leadership."

"Yet how can we know that for sure?" Simpson challenged.

"Because he's still around. He didn't pull his complaint, and he's very specific with his concerns too."

Simpson nodded. "That's true. Yet his motives aren't completely unselfish."

"Fine, he has stock options he wants to protect against bad management. There's nothing wrong with that either. He claims the Kingsleys are putting their employees in danger because they changed leadership to someone inexperienced and inappropriate who altered policies, and their safety practices now don't follow OSHA standards. He states these changes are putting people at risk. That's reason enough to do an investigation. The man didn't even ask for confidentiality."

Kathleen remembered the detailed and painful explanation of how her mother's former employer had exposed her to dangerous chemicals, causing her to contract such rare cancers. It had been hard to take. Hearing Mr. Silva's concerns made Kathleen wonder what might have happened if someone from her mother's company had spoken out against the poor conditions in which they worked. The desire to make someone pay for what happened to her mother fueled Kathleen's desire to act. Her need for revenge became a lifeline, a reason for her to keep breathing every day. Kathleen was determined to make sure no other family would go through what they had. The Winstons lost their matriarch within a year of that conversation.

"How long has he worked for the Kingsleys?"

Kathleen reached for the file that sat on her desk. "Let's see." She flipped through the pages. "Ten years."

"It's only one complaint, but all things considered it would be prudent to do a cursory and very discreet investigation at least. With everything this family has gone through we have got to be careful."

"I can do that," she promised, clapping her hands. "Be discreet and careful, I mean."

"I'm serious, Kathleen. You have to go in under the radar and if—and that's a big *if*—you find anything, then we will bring in the cavalry. I know you're a professional, but you have to make sure your personal feelings and family history of dealing with bad chemical companies don't interfere with you getting the job done…the *right* job."

"I won't," she promised.

"Now, how do you propose to do that?"

"I can go in as one of our policy trainers. Offer them our free services. That always works and will give me access to one of the areas he's complaining about too, not to mention free rein with their staff."

Simpson shook his head. "They train their people themselves. Hell, we even sent some of our trainers to their sessions."

Kathleen tapped her fingers on the desk. "They don't have the new regulatory updates yet. I could offer to go in specifically to talk about them and help update their training materials."

"That might work, but I still need to sweeten the tea." Simpson reached into his pocket, pulled out a Kleenex and wiped his forehead.

"'Sweeten the tea'?" Kathleen held back her laughter. She always found Simpson's use of colloquialisms amusing. "Why?"

"The Kingsleys have been through hell this last year,

and if we're wrong we both could be out of jobs," he informed her, concern written all over his face.

"I'm not wrong, and if I am, I deserve to lose my job."

"Easy for you to say, Kathleen. You've been here seven years, and you come from money. I put in over fifteen years at this agency, and I can't afford to lose my job," Simpson stressed.

Kathleen came from around her desk and leaned against its edge in front of him. She reached for his hand and gave it a quick squeeze. "You won't. I promise. Mr. Silva has no connection to Mr. Perez. There have been a couple of recent changes in their senior management team and policies that have been altered that raised a few eyebrows in the industry. All these changes could be legitimate, but we won't know that for sure unless we check into it. Now how do we sweeten the tea?"

"I'm going to offer our services as a form of an apology for all the false accusations they've had to endure from government agencies as a whole. Show it as a positive PR move on both our parts."

"Do you think that will work?" Kathleen asked, feeling hopeful.

"I guess we'll see." Simpson stood. "I'll let you know after I give their company's chairman of the board and family matriarch, Victoria Kingsley, a call on my way to the doctor's."

"Great. I hope you feel better."

"Talk soon," Simpson said, walking out the office.

The moment the door closed, Kathleen stood in the middle of her office and did a happy dance. "I'm coming for you, Kingsley."

Chapter 2

Morgan Kingsley, the twenty-nine-year-old VP of field operations for Kingsley Oil and Gas, walked into the plant's cafeteria, rubbing his hands together with one thing on his mind: food. It was a room designed to make the Kingsley employees feel at ease and have a sense of home. With all the hours they all spent there away from their families, the Kingsleys felt the least they could do was make sure their employees were comfortable doing their downtime.

He walked into the brightly lit tan-and-white room, which offered various types of wood-and-steel tables paired with large cream leather folding chairs, to find his plant manager, Adrian Jones, standing in the buffet line.

"What are you doing here so early on a Friday, boss?" Adrian asked.

Morgan picked up a tray and plate and surveyed his choices. "I'm about to have breakfast."

"I can see that," Adrian replied, accepting a plate with an omelet from one of the craft service members.

"Lately you've only been around for lunch or dinner."

Skipping the special-order omelet line, Morgan filled his plate with eggs, bacon and pancakes. "Yeah, well, now that all those bogus investigations are over and that bastard Perez is behind bars, I can stay at my own place here and come right to the plant every day and enjoy some of the best breakfast in town."

After spending a few moments at the juice-and-coffee bar, both men made their way to a vacant table. "Cool," Adrian replied, pouring syrup over his stack of pancakes. "You're wearing overalls and work boots. Where are you working today?"

"Maintenance is shorthanded, and I don't want my welders falling behind." Morgan reached for his glass of juice.

"I can pull a couple of people from the south bins to help out."

"That's not necessary. Ernest and I can handle it." Morgan popped a piece of bacon in his mouth.

"Someone call my name?" Ernest Walker, the plant's maintenance director, asked, approaching the table, holding a tray of dirty dishes.

Adrian and Ernest shook hands. "I hear you got the boss doing some heavy lifting today."

"He can handle it," Ernest insisted.

"Damn right," Morgan agreed, diving into his food.

"There you are," a small, gray-haired woman called out as she approached the table, wiping her hands with her apron.

Morgan and Adrian rose from their seats. "Good morning, Ms. Monica," all three men greeted. Ms. Monica, as everyone called her, was the sixty-year-old craft service manager and head chef who had worked for the Kingsleys for nearly thirty years. She was like a grandmother to all the Kingsley boys and pretty much everyone else too.

Ms. Monica was just one of the many reasons Morgan was so happy to have the Perez fiasco behind his family and their business. The plant, located just outside of Port Arthur, Texas, and their oil rigs were his safe haven. The death of his father and uncle were beyond difficult, but his extended family at their plant made growing up without them a bit more bearable.

Often, their mother's love could be suffocating, so when she finally allowed them to spend time at the plant with a few people she trusted who weren't bodyguards, Morgan relished those moments. The plant became his second home and he was fiercely protective of it too.

"We need to talk about the menu that nutritionist lady sent over the other day."

"What's wrong with the menu, Ms. Monica?" Morgan pulled out a chair for her.

Ms. Monica took the seat. "Nothing's wrong with it. Your mother was right. Healthier, balanced diets are something we should all strive for. None of us are getting any younger, you know. In fact, nearly half the folks working have been here since the doors opened. It's just going to be too much money buying so many organic vegetables from that company they recommended. I know where we can get everything we need for much less money. I know y'all rich and all, but it never hurts nobody to save a little money."

Morgan laughed. "You are so right, Ms. Monica, and I appreciate how you look after us—"

"But…" She crossed her arms.

"We have some pretty solid agreements with a number of vendors. Agreements that my mother negotiated personally."

Ms. Monica laughed. "Well, in that case, I'm sure Victoria got you a rock-bottom price."

"Yes, ma'am, I'm sure she did."

"Well, I better get back to my kitchen. It'll be time to serve lunch before I know it. Speaking of lunch, my friend's beautiful daughter—"

"Ms. Monica, we've talked about this already." Morgan helped her out of her chair. *Here we go again. I really wish everyone would stop trying to fix me up. Can't a brother just get back to work and enjoy the fact that no one is coming after us for one thing or another?* "I appreciate your concern, but I don't need help getting dates."

"I'm not trying to help you get hooked up with some hussy," Ms. Monica said and playfully swatted at his hand. Morgan pressed his lips together, preventing his laugh from escaping. "I'm trying to help you find a nice girl you can marry."

"Ms. Monica—"

"And not like that gold digger Bonnie Ford," she continued talking, shaking her head as if he hadn't said a word. "I still can't believe she tried to use your relationship to advance her family's business interest. Ridiculous! Compared to your family's other refineries, that small oil refinery of theirs would look like one of those ugly hateful stepsisters standing next to the beautiful princess. Not to mention all the times he's filed for bankruptcy."

"It was a long time ago," he replied, still feeling a mixture of anger and embarrassment. Morgan had no idea that his three-year, loving relationship with Bonnie—at least he'd thought it was loving—had meant so little to her. He certainly didn't know her and her parents' only agenda for them was to forge a business empire between their families.

"That's my point. It's time for you to stop playing with all these silly little girls and find a woman with some substance. It's time you found yourself a wife."

Morgan checked his watch. "Look at the time. I should get over to the shop."

"Fine, go, but we are not done with this discussion, young man," she insisted, walking toward the kitchen.

Yes, we are. The last thing I need is a wife.

Ms. Monica was like family and Morgan knew she meant well, but he was happy with his life just the way it was. Sexually satisfying liaisons with temporary companions and keeping his heart protected from another bad break suited him just fine. Morgan threw his trash away and set his dishes in the collection pans. He walked toward the exit when his cell phone rang. "Hey, what's up, A?" Morgan answered, stopping shy of the exit.

"China's in labor," Alexander, Morgan's elder brother and CEO of Kingsley Oil and Gas, replied.

"Oh. Snap. Is China all right?"

"She's…emotional but strong," Alexander replied.

"That she is," Morgan agreed.

"And beautiful…so damn beautiful," Alexander murmured.

Morgan heard something in his brother's voice, something unfamiliar. Fear maybe. "Are you okay, A?"

"Yeah, but I could use some backup," he admitted.

"I'm on the way."

"You sure, Morgan?"

"I'm sure. Where am I coming?"

"Woman's Hospital. Thanks, man."

Morgan could hear the relief in his brother's voice. "I'll take the chopper and see you in about an hour."

Morgan put his phone away, pivoted and walked toward another exit, one that would get him to his car the fastest. He still couldn't believe another Kingsley would be arriving soon. Now Morgan had two brothers with children, something he never thought he'd see—so soon, anyway—and briefly wondered if that was a journey he'd ever take.

"I can't believe I let you talk me into this," Kathleen grumbled that night, trying to sit still in the makeup artist's chair. She was anxious to find out if the Kingsley investigation would move forward and kept thinking about all the things that needed to be done before she could get started.

"Like you could go to the Irene Winston Cancer Foundation gala with Dad and me looking like—"

"Like what, Hannah, myself?"

"No, not you. Not the real you, anyway. Maybe a more sedated you," her younger sister conceded.

"I work in the real world where all this excess is not necessary and frowned upon. Just because I don't walk around looking like a glam goddess like you, little sister, Miss TV Chef, doesn't mean I don't look good."

"I didn't say you didn't. What I am saying is that you need to showcase all of our mother's wonderful gifts. The high cheekbones, seductive eyes and—" she ran her hands through her own hair "—all this thick beautiful black hair."

"Hannah, you sound like a beauty commercial," Kathleen said, laughing. "Why aren't Wesley and Kennedy going to this thing tonight?"

"You know our big brother and sister are workaholics just like you. They're out of town on business. Plus they're always at these things. Our foundation's charity events usually have us traveling all over the country. Since this one was local, right in your backyard, we figured you could step up for once," Hannah explained.

"For once?"

"Yes, Kathleen. You rarely make an appearance to any of our social events, be they personal or charitable."

Kathleen bit her lip. "I like my privacy. Besides, my job—"

"Has nothing to do with your family. Stop hiding behind it."

"I'm not," she murmured, knowing her sister was right. Kathleen had enjoyed attending their charitable functions just as much as her sister until their mother got sick. Her mother's illness and trying to find ways to deal with her anger became her focus.

"Whatever. Which dress do you want to wear? They're both Versace." Hannah held up a black, low-backed lace gown in one hand and a red, strapless, flowing gown with a high split in the other. "If I were you—"

"I'll take the black one, please."

"Red, it is," Hannah replied. "You need to show off your banging body and gorgeous face if you want to catch a worthy man."

"I'm not looking for a worthy man, Hannah."

"You should be. You're twenty-nine and haven't had a man since college."

"I've been focusing on my career. Making a difference in people's lives is important to me. I don't need any unnecessary distractions."

"You can still fight your crusade and have a man too. You'd be amazed what great sex can do for a working woman's disposition."

Kathleen rolled her eyes. "My temperament is just fine, thank you very much. Anyway, I don't think there are many men out there like Dad. It would take someone pretty substantial to get me to deviate from my course."

"You won't know until you try and find one," she said challengingly.

"I don't see you running to the altar with Peter."

"And you won't. We've outlived our usefulness for each other," Hannah explained, picking up a comb, running it through her hair and admiring her own beautiful makeup job.

"What? When did that happen?"

"That's a story for another time. You look fabulous." Hannah turned and hugged her makeup artist. "Lisa, you are amazing."

"Thank you, but you both offer a beautiful canvas for my work. I'll see you on the set in the morning. Have a good night, ladies," Lisa said before walking out the door.

"The set?" Kathleen frowned. "I didn't know you were working."

"They booked a couple of promos for me while I'm in town. Houston's one of my biggest markets," she declared proudly.

Kathleen's phone beeped. She reached for it and read the message. A huge smile crawled across her face. Kathleen had just received the go-ahead to go after the Kingsleys. She felt giddy. Like she'd just found out that her favorite book was being turned into a movie. Her boss might believe the Kingsleys were innocent but her gut wouldn't let her join that bandwagon just yet and Kathleen always followed her gut.

"Good news?" Hannah asked.

Curiosity was written all over her sister's face. "The best. I just got my new assignment."

"Oh. Here." Hannah handed Kathleen the red dress, brushing off her news. "Put this one on with the sexy red-and-gold Versace heels I pulled out."

"What are you wearing?"

"Versace, of course, only my dress is a deeper red." Hannah gave her sister a Cheshire cat smile.

"If I didn't know that your IQ was as high as mine or that you were a beast when it came to cooking, I'd swear you were a spoiled, rich woman enamored by the trappings of your lifestyle," Kathleen stated.

Hannah shrugged. "There's nothing wrong with me enjoying the fruits of Dad's and my own labor. Anyway, most of my wardrobe comes to me free."

"Yes, I keep forgetting. People *actually* want to see you in their clothes."

Kathleen walked into her sister's oversize dressing room, dropped her robe and stepped into the gown her sister had selected. It fit her perfectly, accentuating all of her physical assets. Kathleen stared in the full-length mirror and smiled. Her light eyes sparkled, the makeup highlighted her golden-bronze skin beautifully, her black hair full of curls. Kathleen was thankful her hair was pulled up and out of her face.

She hadn't seen the woman staring back at her in quite some time. Not only did she look like a younger, slightly darker version of her mother, which made her both happy and sad, she rarely wore makeup or such fancy clothes anymore. Kathleen only cared about stopping companies from hurting their employees and making the bad guy pay, and she didn't care how she looked doing it. Her heartbeat increased, and she had to fight back her tears. She knew her sister would kill her if she messed up her makeup.

"Ready or not, I'm coming in," Hannah called out before walking into the room. "Oh wow, sis. You look divine…and just like Mom."

Kathleen swallowed hard. The fact that her job didn't require her to dress up was only one reason she didn't like to do it. The other was because it reminded her of just how much she missed her mother. Hannah was right. Irene Winston had blessed her daughters with her beauty.

"So do you," Kathleen replied, smiling at Hannah through the mirror. She turned to face her sister. "I'd say we could pass for twins, except your dress leaves little to the imagination with such a low cut in the front."

Hannah turned around. "And the back," she added, smiling.

Both women laughed. "You are a mess, Hannah."

"I know. Here you go." Hannah handed her sister a black velvet box.

"What's this?" Kathleen's eyebrows snapped together.

"Just a few accessories," she explained.

Kathleen opened the box and her breath caught in her throat. "Oh no, I'm not wearing these." She quickly closed the box and tried to hand it back to her sister. It was like the box held a deadly secret or something. It was one more thing bringing up emotions she was trying to keep buried. The loss of her mother might have fueled her career, but personally it was something she'd never completely dealt with.

"Will you stop being silly? We don't have time to go by your house and get yours so you'll just have to borrow my set tonight."

"That would be a waste of trip since my set isn't at my house," she murmured.

Kathleen heaved a sigh and slowly opened the box as if she'd expected the million-dollar diamond-and-ruby choker and matching stud earrings had disappeared. They had each gotten a set when they'd turned twenty-one. Their father had showered them with jewelry their whole lives. He told them it brought him joy especially since their mother was no longer around to buy things for and spoil.

That was another example as to why Kathleen didn't waste her time dating. There were too many ideals a man would have to live up to, and spoiling her had nothing to do with it. It was the unconditional love that made them want to do such nice and extravagant things for one another. Kathleen just knew that type of love would be hard to find.

"Don't tell me something happened to yours." Fear crossed Hannah's face. "Dad's going to be heartbroken."

Kathleen frowned at Hannah as she reached for the earrings. "Don't be silly. Most of my jewelry is in my safety deposit box. I only keep a few pieces in my home safe." She removed the necklace from the box and placed it around her neck.

"Why not keep all your stuff in your home safe?"

"Because it's not like I wear so much jewelry every day."

"Good point." Hannah adjusted her diamond necklace. "How's work going anyway? I know you can't tell me who you're going after but whoever it is had better watch out."

Kathleen smiled. She had gone up against some powerful people in her career and while ambition had never been a motivating factor for Kathleen, she knew bringing down the Kingsleys would be a big feather in her career cap. "Let's just say it's a really big fish that I can't wait to catch and fry."

"You go, girl. Ready? I just got a text. Dad's here, and you know how he feels about being late." Kathleen heard her phone beep. She knew she'd just received the same message. "You ready to spend your Friday night with Dad?"

"I might as well be." Kathleen gave herself one final look in the mirror and smiled. She knew how much her mother had loved to dress up and that she'd be really happy right now. "Let's go celebrate Mom and raise a lot of money for cancer research." *Tomorrow I'll start the process of bringing down another company that won't make the safety of their employees a priority.*

Chapter 3

After an eventful weekend, Morgan walked into the plant's operations director's office, drinking from his travel mug, to find his mother standing in the middle of the room looking out the window. She was wearing a blue pantsuit that showed off how physically fit she was, emphasizing the fact that age was nothing but a number. Her bag sat on the desk next to her personalized hard hat.

"Mother, what are you doing here?" Morgan asked, checking his watch. His mother wasn't exactly a morning person these days, so he was trying not to let her unexpected visit concern him, but the last couple of times she'd surprised him it had been to share bad news.

Morgan was actually looking forward to getting back to work and focusing on expanding into new territories—all the things he'd been working on before Perez entered into their lives. Still reeling from the excitement of the weekend, the birth of another Kingsley and seeing how happy his brothers were, Morgan was actually considering taking Ms. Monica up on her offer to introduce him to her friend's daughter. Although he knew that particular thought would soon pass.

Victoria turned and faced Morgan. "Good morning, son. I realize we've had an exciting weekend and that you might be a little out of sorts on this bright Monday morning, but I'm sure you haven't forgotten the appropriate way to greet your mother."

Morgan sighed and placed his cup on the desk next to his mother's hat. He leaned in and kissed her on the cheek. "My apologies. Good morning, and to what do I owe the pleasure of this visit? Is everything good with Baby A?" His heart skipped several beats at the thought that something could be wrong with his new nephew. Morgan never imagined that something so small could knock him off balance and make him feel so much.

Victoria's face lit up with pride. "Alexander the third is wonderful," she reassured, smiling, taking a seat in front of the desk. "I'm here because with all the excitement around little Alexander's birth this weekend I failed to mention that you'll be receiving a visitor today."

"A visitor?" He reached for his coffee.

"Yes. I got a call Friday afternoon from another one of my well-placed sources in our state government offering me a few olive branches so to speak for all the trouble we've…our company had to endure this last year."

"Oh, really, what type of olive branch?" Morgan questioned, narrowing his eyes while the hairs on the back of his neck rose. At this point Morgan didn't trust anyone from any government agency.

"The only one you need to worry about is the one from OSHA. They're sending one of their trainers to update our material and orientate our employees on some new regulatory updates."

"They're what?" Morgan frowned. *Why in the hell would I need or want to use any of their trainers?*

"You heard me, son."

Morgan went around the desk and dropped down in the chair. He knew better than to argue with his mother about the decisions she made for the company, especially those that might have political ramifications. He had to pick his words carefully.

"Do you really want someone from any government agency in our business after everything we've been through? I certainly don't. I can send a couple of our trainers for a train-the-trainer session and they can come back and train everyone else here. You realize they send their trainers to our training center for a number of different programs we conduct?" he reminded his mother, trying to keep his annoyance under control.

"I do, son, and while that sounds like a great idea, unfortunately I've already agreed and given my word."

Morgan gave his head a quick shake. "When will they get here?"

Victoria gave a nonchalant shrug. "I have no idea. All I know is that they arrive today."

Morgan grabbed his cup and took a sip. "I'll listen to what they have to offer, but if it's not up to our standards, the ones you set, I'll send them packing."

Victoria rose from her seat and smiled. "I wouldn't expect anything less. Now, let's go." She reached for her hard hat.

Morgan stood. "Where are we going?"

"To talk to some of the line staff. It's been a while since I've been out here. I'd like to see a few people.

Just deliver me to Adrian, and you can wait for our guest in his office."

"Yes, ma'am." Morgan offered her his arm, and they walked out of the office.

Kathleen arrived at the Kingsley plant close to ten, much later than she would have liked thanks to an unexpected traffic jam on the freeway. She was impressed by the level of security just to gain entrance to the property and the plant itself, although part of her wondered if that was a sign that the Kingsleys were trying to hide something. Kathleen exited her vehicle, pulled out her roller bag and purse and made her way to the guard's stand.

"Good morning, ma'am. May I help you?" one of the three guards greeted.

"Yes." Kathleen pulled out her ID and flashed it to the guard. "I'm Kathleen Winston from OSHA, and I'm here to conduct some training sessions."

"One moment." The officer reached for his phone at the same time Kathleen's rang. She checked the screen and saw that it was her father calling. Instead of answering she sent him to voice mail.

The guard handed Kathleen a visitor's badge. "You'll need to keep this on you at all times. Please follow me. May I help you with your bag?"

"No, thanks. I have it."

Kathleen followed her escort over to a small truck. He handed her a hard hat. "You need to put this on." He gave her the once over, and the corners of his mouth turned down as he nodded.

"Is everything okay?"

"Yes, ma'am. It's just most of our female visitors don't think to wear sensible shoes like the ones you're wearing."

Kathleen looked down, past the conservative black suit and white blouse she wore to the black leather loafers on her feet, and laughed. "This isn't my first time working in a plant." She got in the truck and watched the guard load her things while she put on the hat. Kathleen was glad she'd remembered to put her hair in a low, tight bun when she got dressed.

"My name is Van, ma'am," the guard stated as he got in the truck behind the wheel.

"Pleased to meet you," she replied, smiling.

Van gave Kathleen a map of the plant in the form of a brochure before giving her the layout as he drove around the outskirts. He highlighted the major points of interest. Van explained that she'd have to have an escort to each location.

"Will you be that escort?"

"No, ma'am. That will either be the plant manager, Adrian Jones, or someone he assigns."

Kathleen had done her research and she knew all the names of the key staff and the positions they held at the plant; however, several of their photos hadn't been available. She especially found it surprising how little she was able to find out about the Kingsleys. Yes, there was a great deal of detail about their recent troubles, their financial fortune and of course their family's matriarchs, but minimal information beyond tabloid gossip was available about the personal lives of the heirs.

They drove toward a large one-story white building with the Kingsley name on it. "Is that where I'm going?"

"At some point I'm sure. That's the administrative building where you'll find the training center. However, I was told to bring you to the plant manager's office."

They rode in silence through the middle of the plant on what was a main street, and Kathleen was surprised to see a five-story glass office building surrounded by several other equally impressive buildings of varying sizes positioned in the center of the plant. *Wow. You can't judge a book by its cover but this place is pretty great.* "This plant is like a small town."

"You haven't seen anything yet. The Kingsleys take good care of their people." They pulled into an assigned parking space and exited the truck.

I'll keep that in mind.

Kathleen collected her things and followed Van into the building where another security guard met them. Before the guard could offer a greeting, a tall Hispanic man wearing jeans and a white button-down shirt with Kingsley Oil and Gas monogrammed above his left shirt pocket said, "Good morning, Ms. Winston. I'm Paz Villarreal, operations manager." He offered her his hand.

"Pleased to meet you," she replied, accepting his callus-riddled hand, and smiled.

"Thanks, I got it," he told the officer from his building as he patted him on the back. "Thanks, Van, I got it from here. You can get back to your post."

He nodded. "Thank you, Van," Kathleen said.

"No problem, ma'am."

"May I help you with your bag?" Paz offered.

"No, thank you. I'm fine. We passed your training center coming in. Will I not be working there?"

"Eventually." They walked over to the elevator and took the short ride up to the fifth floor. He led her past a small waiting area and down a long hall with offices on each side. They came to the end of the hall and stood in front of a door with a sign that read Operations Administration. Paz opened the door and stood aside as Kathleen entered. It wasn't at all what she'd expected. The waiting area had two low-back leather sofas sitting against the left and right walls with framed blueprints of the plant hanging above them. An expensive Persian rug covered the slate floors, and a long fish tank filled the back wall.

"Very nice."

Paz laughed. "You haven't seen anything yet. Follow me." He led her toward a door in the corner.

Kathleen's forehead creased. "No receptionist?"

"It's not necessary. You can't get up here without an escort unless you're an employee or a Kingsley." He led her through the door.

Time to get to work. "I was wondering, are they here often…the Kingsleys?" She gave him a half smile.

"Sure."

"How involved are they with the staff? I mean, do they spend much time with the employees? What do they do while they're here?" Kathleen tried not to sound like she was going down a checklist but she knew she was failing in that effort. She prayed her face didn't show how unsettled she was. It was not as if this was the first time she had to come into a facility incognito to find out what was going on, but something felt different about this one. Her boss was right—the Kingsleys were a big deal—and she couldn't mess this up. Kathleen knew the outcome of her investigation could have far-reaching ramifications.

Paz looked at Kathleen as if she was speaking a foreign language and he didn't understand a word she was saying. "They work just like the rest of us," he replied, frowning.

They walked down another corridor, passing several more offices until they made it to the large double doors at the end of the hall. "You can wait in here, and Mr. Jones will be right with you." Paz opened the door, and Kathleen walked in, stopping before she could get more than a foot into the room.

"Back again, Adrian?" a baritone voice said, sending an unfamiliar chill down Kathleen's spine. The sound came from a olive-skinned man with a short haircut and a fine beard. His long jean-clad legs were propped up on the desk, and he was reading through what appeared to be a report. When he raised his head, and Kathleen caught his gaze, his hazel eyes rendered her mute. Kathleen's throat was suddenly dry, and she blinked rapidly. The short-sleeved white shirt he wore with the company's logo on the pocket accentuated his wide chest and big arms.

"Oh my," she whispered to herself. Kathleen had seen handsome men before, but this man was unlike any of those. The ruggedly handsome gentleman sitting before her looked like someone from one of the old black-and-white Westerns she and her mother used to enjoy watching together. Her mother would tell Kathleen, "That's what a man's man is, darling," when one appeared on the screen. Today was the first time she'd seen one in person, and the thought made Kathleen smile.

Morgan slowly lowered his papers to the desk, brought his feet to the floor and stood. He felt like his whole body was moving in slow motion. Morgan had seen beautiful women before, but the exquisite creature standing in front of him was different. Her heart-shaped face and flawless skin was mostly makeup free. She appeared to be a foot or so shorter than Morgan; her smile was faint but stunning, and while she tried to cover her perfectly shaped body in conservative clothes, Morgan could see that she had curves in all the right places that called out to him, and his body was responding. It was something that never happened by the sight of a woman.

Damn!

Paz stepped forward. "This is Kathleen Winston. Kathleen, this is—"

He raised his left hand and waved him off. Morgan hadn't heard anything beyond her name. What he didn't recognize were the emotions she had provoked in him. He felt warm, he couldn't seem to focus and he had a sudden desire to touch her. He'd heard about this happening before, only he was usually watching from the sideline of his brothers' lives.

Morgan quickly righted himself. "You must be the trainer from OSHA," Morgan forced out, extending his hand. "I'm—"

"Yes," Kathleen interrupted, offering her hand.

Morgan felt a spark as he gave her small, delicate hand a shake. *Get it together.* "Excuse the calluses."

Kathleen smiled, sending another spark through his body, the sweet scent she was wearing attacking his senses. "No problem." She freed her hand.

"May I?" She gestured toward one of the two large leather wingback chairs that sat in front of the mahogany wood desk.

"Please."

Morgan returned to his seat and watched as Kathleen quickly removed four medium-sized binders from her bag and placed them on the desk. He told himself he would listen to what she had to say, but he would send her away as soon as she read her last page. There was no way in hell this beautiful woman could teach anything to his men. They wouldn't be able to concentrate. He sure as hell couldn't right then.

Kathleen removed her electronic tablet from her bag and turned it on. She handed Morgan a binder and said, "I've taken the liberty of highlighting a few deficiencies in your training program."

"Deficiencies?" Morgan sat forward and opened the binder, feeling annoyed by her assumption in spite of being so turned on by her presence.

"The first tab has my résumé and all my credentials and certifications. If you look behind the second tab, you'll find my recommendations for improvement," Kathleen explained.

"That was mighty presumptuous of you, considering the state uses our material as part of its training program." He hardened his expression as he glanced down at the pages.

"Not really. It's my job to ensure all safety protocols are adhered to regardless of whose name is on the building.

"I—"

"Look, I'm sure you're loyal to the Kingsley family." She shook her head as if that was the most ridiculous thing she'd ever heard.

"You have no idea," Morgan replied.

"However there are some things where loyalty isn't a part of the equation."

That was when Morgan realized she had no idea who she was talking to. He remembered that she'd launched into her presentation before he had a chance to introduce himself. *She's arrogant and another know-it-all when it comes to my family.* "In my mind and my family's, loyalty is everything."

"This isn't about you or your family. Making improvements to your systems is about protecting you and your coworkers. Shall I continue?" Kathleen's eyebrows stood at attention.

The girl's got spunk. The way her eyes bored into him was wreaking havoc on his system. Morgan folded his arms across his chest. "Please."

Chapter 4

Morgan sat back and watched Kathleen make her presentation as he flipped through the pages of her binder ahead of her. He tried to focus on her words, but her green-gold eyes and luscious lips scrambled his brain. Only a few phases broke through the fog of annoyance and attraction, one of which he had to address.

"Wait, did you say we need to switch from our computer-based training program to a more group-based, interactive one?" *That's not going to happen.* "The industry, the world for that matter, is moving more toward digital and you want us to pull back."

"Yes, statistics show people respond better in a working group setting like the one I'm recommending. They learn from their peers, and it strengthens relationships between coworkers."

Morgan dropped his hands. "My team already works well together. They don't need a feel-good session to make them better at their job." He closed the binder. "Stick to the regulatory updates, and I'll make sure our systems are brought current based on those changes."

Kathleen raised her chin and held his gaze. "While I appreciate your opinion, it doesn't count, Mr. Jones."

"What do we have here?" Victoria asked as she entered the office with Adrian on her heels. She placed her hat back on the desk.

Morgan and Kathleen got to their feet. "Victoria Kingsley, meet Kathleen Winston, the trainer OSHA sent."

Victoria extended her hand. "Pleased to meet you, and welcome to Kingsley Oil and Gas. I take it things are going well."

"Not exactly," Morgan stated.

Unfortunately, thanks to Mr. Tall, Handsome and Too-Damn-Sexy-for-His-Own-Good.

"Miss Winston seems to think we should abandon our tried-and-true computer-based training in favor of her more interactive-type program," Morgan explained. His jaw tightened.

Kathleen glared at Morgan before turning her attention to Victoria. "It's not my program, and I didn't suggest you abandon your computer-based training altogether—just adjust it a bit."

"A bit." Morgan pointed to the binders that sat on his desk. "According to the data in your unnecessarily long, although well-put-together, presentation, you recommend we cut our program by fifty percent."

"And replace it with a more productive method of training," she countered.

"Says you." Morgan crossed his arms.

"Says several experts. How did you even see that? We haven't even gotten to that section yet." Kathleen made her annoyance clear. She thought he was acting like a petulant child.

I bet you stomp your feet and hold your breath, too, if a woman doesn't drop to her knees on command. Oh, my goodness. Where the hell did that come from, Kathleen?

"I'm good at multitasking, and I pay attention to details."

Another warm sensation ran through her body. "I bet you do," she murmured.

Victoria laughed as she reached for her buzzing phone. "Well, I see you have everything under control, son." She started reading her incoming text.

"'Son'?" Kathleen's forehead creased; she was clearly shocked by the revelation. "I thought you were the plant manager."

"No, that would be me," another man replied, raising his right hand.

Victoria placed her hands on her hips. "Morgan Kingsley, did you not properly introduce yourself to this young woman?"

"I tried, but she launched right into her presentation. I think she was a bit awestruck." Morgan smirked.

Kathleen's left eyebrow rose. "As were you," she snapped back before she could stop herself.

"Touché," Morgan acknowledged.

"Enough." Victoria picked up her bag and hard hat. "I have to get back to Houston."

Morgan dropped his hands. "I'll see you out, Mother."

"No, Adrian will. You and Miss Winston are going to get to work." Victoria turned and faced Kathleen. "While I appreciate your input and we will take your recommendations under advisement, we will continue to do what we feel is best for our company. If you can't accept that, I have to rescind my offer to allow your presence at my plant."

That can't happen. "Yes, of course. I understand," she replied nervously.

"Good, now pass me one of those binders, and I'll read through it on the ride home."

Nice going, Kathleen—you almost get yourself kicked out of here before you can even get started. Kathleen handed Victoria a binder and watched as she kissed her son goodbye and left. She had heard and read a great deal about Victoria Kingsley but nothing compared to meeting her in person. While she was very firm and definitive in regard to her business, watching her maternal interactions with her son was something clearly not many got to witness. She felt honored.

"Well, I guess that's that." Kathleen started packing up her bag. "I'll focus on the regulatory changes as you requested, Mr. Kingsley."

Kathleen watched the handsome Kingsley drop his shoulders and lean against his desk. The closer he got to Kathleen, the more out of control she felt. Kathleen knew she had to bring her wayward mind and body under control. He was part of her investigation, after all.

"It's Morgan, and if you prefer you can conduct your sessions using your interactive method. If the team is receptive to the idea, I'll consider incorporating your way into *some* of our program."

Kathleen offered up a small smile. "Was that too hard?"

"Not at all. I can be a reasonable man when I want to be, Miss Winston."

"I guess we'll find out just how reasonable you are when you attend my class, and please call me Kathleen."

"All right, Kathleen, but I have no intention of attending your class," he said matter-of-factly.

Kathleen felt a slow smile spread across her face. "Why? Are you afraid you just might learn something and realize my method is better than the program you so covet?"

"Not at all." His face went blank, and he held her gaze.

Kathleen dropped her eyes and reached for her rolling bag. "Shall I get started?"

"Absolutely."

Morgan came from around the desk and reached for Kathleen's bag. "I got it," she said.

"I insist," he replied as he placed his large hand over hers.

Kathleen felt a spark that wasn't electrical and quickly pulled her hand back. *You have got to get it together.* "Fine."

"And if I may suggest…you are open to suggestions, right?"

Annoyed by the sarcasm, Kathleen rolled her eyes. "Yes, of course."

"You should lose whatever that perfume is you're wearing. The men might find it distracting if you want them to focus on your class. Don't worry—they'd never be inappropriate."

"I'm not, and I know the drill. Besides, I'm not wearing perfume," Kathleen explained, walking toward the door.

Morgan stepped in her path, preventing Kathleen from moving forward. He stared into her eyes and said, "If you're not wearing perfume, then it's you. All you," he concluded, his voice low and husky.

Kathleen felt light-headed. She thought for a moment

that somehow all the oxygen had been sucked out of the room. *Focus, Kathleen.*

"I want my men to concentrate on the training and not the trainer," he continued.

Kathleen pushed her shoulders back and raised her chin defiantly. "Maybe it's you with the concentration problem. Every consider leading by example?" She stepped around him and walked out the door.

Kathleen's first day wasn't as difficult as she'd imagined. It was just the opposite. Everyone was extremely nice but not in a sucking-up type of way, either. The assistance offered to Kathleen no matter where she went or what she requested was unlike anything she'd ever experienced. Everyone seemed genuinely happy to help. Even her initial class, in which she'd expected to receive pushback, especially from the more seasoned staff, went well. Everyone appeared open to the training, and some were even excited about the opportunity to explore her new methods. Other than that initial hiccup in the office that morning, she had a good day. Kathleen still couldn't get over the effect Morgan Kingsley had on her mind and body. Her attraction to him was an unexpected hurdle she had to get over. The jury was still out on Morgan and his company.

While Kathleen had limited access to the Kingsley systems, she was given the ability to review all the training material including their archived programs. A big part of Mr. Silva's charge had been that the new COO had implemented policy changes that put the staff in danger. Kathleen was in the perfect position to prove or disprove that allegation. The first thing she did was check the company's policy change log against what they had filed with the state. She found no irregulari-

ties. In fact, she was impressed with just how well orga-
nized they were. However, Kathleen knew just because
the paperwork was in order didn't mean everything
was aboveboard. Yet for some reason she felt relieved
that the paperwork confirmed what she'd seen so far.
It was like she was rooting for them, which was something that she never did this early in the investigation.

Employers often put one thing in writing but expected their employees to cut corners to get the job
done faster and cheaper, regardless of the potential
risk to themselves and their families. Most employees went along with such antics because they felt they
had no choice. Kathleen was determined to make sure
the Kingsley employees knew they had a choice. Over
the next couple of weeks, Kathleen conducted what
she called "featherlight interviews" with her trainees. She would weave investigative questions into her
training sessions and found nothing out of the ordinary.
While Kathleen appreciated his hands-off approach to
her work, she found herself looking forward to their
check-in moments, as Morgan called them, at the end
of each day.

But Kathleen combed through old and new training records and found a smoking gun. Unfortunately,
it wasn't what she'd expected. The most damaging evidence she found was against a senior-level welder by
the name of Mundos Silva. While Kathleen couldn't review the Kingsley employees' personal records, she did
have access to their training files. It seems Mr. Mundos
Silva had experienced a great deal of difficulty passing
most of his required training. It had taken him longer
than others and multiple times to pass. There were notes
in his files indicating that his supervisors had offered
him assistance and additional training in areas where

he was having difficulty. Unfortunately, Mr. Silva refused the help. Kathleen found that the outside training specialist recommended that Mr. Silva be demoted to a position more appropriate for his current level of ability. The recommendation and change took effect long before there was a change in leadership.

"Damn," Kathleen replied, after reading the last note in his file. She called her boss.

"Kathleen, what's up?" Simpson answered.

"I found something."

"What?" She could hear the anxiousness in his voice.

"It's not against the Kingsleys, but Mr. Silva."

"Tell me."

After going over everything she'd found out so far, she read the final note in the file. "'Mr. Silva is a valued employee who we should do everything we can to try to help according to the Kingsley Family Stay Whole policy.'"

"What the hell is the Kingsley Family Stay Whole policy?" he asked.

"Apparently anyone who's been here for more than five years is eligible to receive any form of help they may need in the event of a crisis, to stay whole."

"What?"

"I just heard about it. The Kingsleys believe in taking care of their employees. There's even something for those who've been here for fewer than five years," she added.

"Maybe we can get a job there after we're both fired. It's time to come home, Kathleen."

"Not yet. You need to bring Mr. Silva in for a follow-up conversation."

Kathleen was experiencing a whirlwind of emotions. Confusion and anger that she might have let herself get played and pleasure that it appeared the Kingsleys were actually what she was finding them to be: good people with a great company.

"I'm already ahead of you, but there's nothing to find," Simpson insisted.

"You may be right, but I have to be sure. Besides, I have to finish the training and system updates. That way I can leave, and no one will ever know the real reason for my visit."

"Fine, but make it fast," he said before hanging up on her.

Kathleen had a feeling that Simpson was right, but for reasons she didn't want to explore she just knew she had to stay a little longer…for Morgan.

Chapter 5

The pledge that Morgan made to keep his distance proved to be harder than he thought. He spent the next two weeks doing everything he could to avoid spending any time alone with Kathleen. Whenever she came near him with questions, concerns or comments his brain seem to shut down, allowing his hormones to take control. After turning down several recent offers for female companionship, putting himself through grueling workouts in his home gym and riding his horses until he started to smell like one himself, Morgan spent the entire weekend wondering what Kathleen was doing. She never wore rings, so he figured she wasn't married, but it seemed impossible for a woman like that to be single. The question and idea had made him nuts all weekend.

Morgan had a history of dating beautiful and compliant women, but none of them affected him like Kathleen. Her beauty aside, it was her passion for her work, the compassion he'd seen her show his team, but most of all, the way she challenged him when she believed she was right about something that attracted him.

It was another Monday afternoon when Morgan sat

at a table in the cafeteria across from where Kathleen was sitting talking to several of his employees. However, this time she seemed to be focusing her attention on Troy, one of his senior welders. The way she threw her head back when she laughed at whatever he was saying to her grated at him and he had no idea why.

"I'm surprised Kathleen hasn't filed charges against you," Adrian said before biting into his chicken.

"What?" Morgan frowned and he looked over at his friend.

Adrian wiped his mouth with his napkin and said, "The way you're attacking her with those glares."

Morgan turned his head and pushed his plate forward. "I don't know what you're talking about."

"Sure you do. Just ask Kathleen out already," Adrian suggested.

"Don't be ridiculous. First, Kathleen works here. Second, she may be married or at least have a man. And third, I'm not—"

"Don't say you're not interested because I know better."

"Do you now?"

"We've been friends for over ten years, and I know when someone's piqued your interest. Considering all the hard labor you've put in these last couple weeks, I'd say Kathleen has more than done that."

What she's doing is driving me crazy. "Like I said, she works here—"

"She's working here. She doesn't *work* here, and as far as her being married or having a man, she isn't, and she doesn't."

Morgan could feel his anger on the rise, and he didn't understand why. Had Adrian asked Kathleen out? Did she turn him down? Had he already gone out with her?

Those questions were racing through his mind and driving him crazy. "How the hell do you know that?"

Adrian must have sensed the change in Morgan's demeanor. "Chill, man, I heard one of the welding guys asked her out."

"Who?" Morgan hadn't realized that he'd fisted his hands on the table.

Adrian shrugged and took another bite of his food. "I'm not sure, but I think it might be one of the guys she's sitting next to. I don't know if she said yes."

I'm going to fire his ass. Wait, where the hell did that come from? He used the palm of his right hand to rub against his temple.

Adrian turned toward his friend. "Look, man, just ask the woman out. You know you want to. Didn't you say she seemed interested when you first met?"

"Yeah, when she thought she was talking to you. Ever since she found out who I was, Kathleen's been tense and standoffish."

"Probably because you've been quiet and brooding." Adrian wiped his face and took a drink of his soda.

"Quiet and brooding?"

"Yeah, that's what the women around here call you," Adrian explained with a half smile.

"Do they now?"

"Yes. You haven't even attended one of Kathleen's classes," Adrian noted.

"I don't need to," he defended.

"She might appreciate the gesture, and you'd be surprised how cool it is."

Morgan's eyebrows rose. "Would I?"

"Hell, perhaps Kathleen would like a man who can make her laugh like that." Adrian directed Morgan's attention to the area were Kathleen now stood talking to Troy and two additional women. They were all laughing and standing near the exit, and Kathleen had her hand resting on Troy's arm.

"Perhaps we should both get back to work. Those containers aren't going to clean themselves."

Morgan stood, threw his trash out and headed for the exit away from where Kathleen stood. Morgan knew Adrian was right, he couldn't stop thinking about her, but he also knew he had to get his foreign and inconvenient feelings for Kathleen under control before he did anything. It was time to talk to one of his brothers, and he knew the perfect one too.

Kathleen had been keeping an eye on Morgan from the moment he walked into the cafeteria. Their encounters over the last couple of weeks were very professional, although she found herself having more inappropriate thoughts and dreams about the man she was investigating, a probe that had only yielded positive responses from his employees.

As part of her investigation, she got to see how well prepared his administrative team as well as his frontline staff were. Kathleen needed to make sure she wasn't allowing her personal whatever she was feeling for Morgan to interfere with her ability to do her job. It had never been a problem before, and she was going to make sure it didn't become one now. It was time to deal with Morgan Kingsley.

Kathleen figured if she could interview him about the complaint one of two things would happen. She'd either be able to clear the charges once and for all or find a reason to move forward with a full investigation. Now all she had to do was find a way to interview Morgan without him catching on. Kathleen knew just the person to ask for help too.

Morgan stood in the immaculately decorated living room of his younger brother Brice's home and smiled. He remembered how not very long ago when he'd visited his brother, Brice would direct him downstairs to his man cave and away from the living room. The painful memories of his then soon-to-be ex-wife were too much to handle. Morgan was happy his brother and sister-in-law had since reconciled, even though at first he hadn't seen it happening. Watching Brice handle his conflicting feelings for Brooke while being forced to work with her told Morgan that Brice would be the perfect person to ask about his foreign feelings for Kathleen and how best to handle them.

"Here you go." Brice handed Morgan a bottle of beer.

"Thanks, man. You sure this is cool? I haven't interrupted anything, have I?" he asked, noticing his brother's wet hair, pajama bottoms and T-shirt.

"Not now," he replied, smiling.

"Good, I'd hate to disturb Brooke. How's she doing with everything?"

"She's fine. She hasn't had an MS flare-up in a while."

"That's great. I still can't get over how well you two are handing Brooke's multiple sclerosis diagnosis. I'm proud of you, bro."

"I appreciate that. We've made a decision."

"About what?"

Brice's face lit up. "We selected a surrogate, and we're starting the process next week."

"For real?"

"Yep." Brice nodded.

Morgan hugged his brother. "Congratulations, man. I know how much you want kids, but I also know how much you need to keep Brooke safe." He took a long pull from his bottle as he watched Brice's expression morph from happiness to fear back to happiness again in the matter of seconds.

"Let's sit down."

Morgan took a seat in one of the two large wingback chairs across from his brother, who was now sitting on a sofa. "Have you shared it with the rest of the family?"

"No. You're the first. Mother won't be surprised, since she's the one who made the recommendation and found us the perfect agency."

"Why am I not surprised?" Morgan took another drink from his bottle.

"Because she's Victoria Kingsley. Now, what brings you out here? You were all cryptic when you called," he asked, finally getting around to taking a drink from his beer bottle.

Morgan placed his now empty bottle on the coffee table. He leaned forward, resting his forearms on his thighs, clasping his hands. "There's this woman—"

"Oh wow...wait." Brice held up his left hand and put his beer bottle down on the floor. "You came to see me about a woman?"

"Yeah, so..."

Brice clapped his hands and started laughing. Morgan knew he deserved his brothers' ribbing after all the hard times he'd given all of them about their problems with women while he incessantly played the field after Bonnie broke his heart, but now really wasn't the time. He needed his help. Morgan sat back in the chair. "You done?"

"Sorry, man. I'm done. What's going on and who is this woman who has finally got Morgan Kingsley, the king of the bachelors, Mister No-Woman's-Worth-the-Drama all twisted up in his feelings?"

"Her name is Kathleen Winston—"

"The trainer from OSHA?" Brice frowned.

Morgan rose from his seat. "That's the one."

"Damn, man, she just got there, and you've already—"

"No, I haven't." Morgan started a slow pace around the room. "I haven't done anything, and that's the problem."

"I don't understand."

Morgan released an audible sigh. "Neither do I, which is why I'm here. So, what do I do?"

Brice frowned. "About what?"

"Men…" a small, soft voice called out as Brooke descended the stairs and entered the living room, barefoot and wearing a robe.

Morgan stopped midstride, and Brice stood. He reached for his wife's hand and pulled her into his arms, kissing her on the cheek. "Sorry if we disturbed you, sweetheart," Brice stated.

A warm feeling came over Morgan watching the sweet exchange, and while normally such a sight never affected him, he was finding himself thinking about how nice it would be to have such a moment, maybe with a beautiful stranger who he couldn't even have a real conversation with.

"Yeah, sorry about that, sister-in-law."

"Don't be silly—you didn't disturb me. I was ear hustling from the top of the stairs, and I couldn't take it anymore."

Brice laughed. "You were eavesdropping?"

"Well, yeah. It's rare that Morgan comes to anyone for help about anything and I knew it couldn't be about business this late. I figured it had to be good." Brook cupped Brice's face with her right hand. "I love you, sweetheart, but you suck at translating stories."

"True," Brice agreed.

"I knew if I wanted to find out what was going on I'd better find out for myself," Brooke confessed.

While the exchange between his brother and sister-in-law was cute, it wasn't helping him at the moment. "I should probably go," Morgan stated, moving toward the door.

"You will do no such thing. Sit…both of you," Brooke ordered, taking the twin chair next to Morgan. She angled her body toward him. "Let me see if I got this right. You've developed feelings for the OSHA trainer. You're not sure if you should act on them nor are you sure that you can't either. Is that the gist of the situation?"

Morgan smirked. "That about covers it. Except I can't seem to stop thinking about her or putting my foot in my mouth whenever I'm around her."

"Damn…you got it bad," Brice teased.

"Stop it," Brooke chastised her husband. "You've never had trouble talking to women. I'm sure she's beautiful," Brooke suggested.

"Breathtakingly so," Morgan confirmed.

"And that's never been a problem either. What makes this one so different?" Brooke's eyebrows came together.

Brooke's apparent confusion merely matched his own. Morgan leaned forward again and briefly lowered his eyes to the floor before returning his attention to his sister-in-law. "She's so much more. It's not just her looks. I've seen her be strong and she won't take crap from me or any of those roughnecks around the plant. Talk about smart. Kathleen has an impeccable résumé and she knows the ins and outs of the oil and gas business. Talking business with her is like talking to one of you, which is why everyone seems to respect her so much." He felt two sets of eyes bore into his face.

"Wow. I wasn't sure I'd live to see the day," Brice said in a hushed tone.

"I was," Brooke acknowledged, smiling.

"What are you two talking about?" Morgan's frustration with himself and his family was rising. He needed answers.

"You're falling in love," Brice stated.

"I'd say he's already fallen," Brooke corrected.

"No… I'm not. Hell, I can't even talk to her," Morgan declared.

"We know," the two replied in unison.

"Look, Morgan, just ask her out. I bet you'll be surprised to find that she's into you too."

"At first I thought she might be until she found out who I was," Morgan informed, feeling annoyed with himself and remembering the moment.

Brooke's forehead creased. "What does that mean?"

After explaining his first encounter with Kathleen, Morgan added, "Ever since that day, things have been just professional."

Brooke rose from her chair, and Morgan and Brice mimicked her move. "You're a smart guy with a good heart. Show that side of yourself to her. Find a way to push past your fear and think of a clever way to ask her out. Life is too short to miss out on or run away from…" Brooke's eyes cut to her husband briefly before landing back on Morgan "…any opportunity that could change your life and bring you untold happiness."

Morgan hugged Brooke. "Thank you. My brother is one lucky man."

"We're both lucky." Brooke kissed Brice before she headed back upstairs.

"She's right, you know," Brice added.

Morgan shoved his hands in his pockets. He still couldn't believe how twisted his insides were behind a woman he'd spent nearly no time with at all. "I know she is, but I still don't know what to do about it."

"You can start by taking a nonjudgmental interest in what her training program has to offer."

Morgan glared at Brice. "You think I should sit through her touchy-feely training to do what? Get her to like me…to go out with me?"

"If that's what you want. *Is* that what you want?"

Morgan stared at his brother but held his tongue while his body stirred, making its opinion known. "Thanks, man. I'm going to head out."

"Anytime."

Morgan walked out Brice's door, contemplating the answer to his brother's question. He knew what he wanted and what he had to do to get it.

Kathleen sat with her back against the headboard of the king-size bed in her Port Arthur hotel room. The entire room was half the size of her bedroom at home, but Kathleen didn't mind. She never reveled in her wealth and privilege, unlike her siblings. Kathleen spent most of her time focusing on righting perceived injustices in the world within her reach. Although she did have one vice: collecting art, antiques specifically.

Having just showered and changed into a long nightshirt, Kathleen settled in for the night. When her phone rang, she stared down at the screen and froze. Morgan Kingsley was calling her. Kathleen wasn't sure if she should answer it or send him to voice mail but before she could decide the ringing stopped. A feeling of disappointment came over Kathleen until her phone beeped, alerting her to a newly received message. Her disappointment quickly was replaced by a mixture of excitement and fear. Kathleen pushed out a quick breath and played back the message.

"Good evening, Miss Winston. This is Morgan Kingsley. Forgive the intrusion, but I want you to know that I'll be joining your training session in the morning. See you tomorrow."

Morgan's smooth, baritone voice sent a warm feeling throughout her body. Kathleen replayed the message several times, not because it wasn't clear, but because she was enjoying what his voice was doing to her body, specifically to the lower half of her sexually deprived body. All of her fantasies about Morgan were closing in on her.

Kathleen closed her eyes and ran her right hand across her breasts and down her stomach to her sex. Morgan's handsome face and the sound of his voice filled Kathleen's mind. Her hand slipped under her panties and slid through the fine hairs to her core. She lay flat on her back, spread her legs and inserted one, then two fingers inside as she thought about Morgan and all the sexy things they could do together. Before long she'd found temporary relief to desires he'd managed to tap into.

"You've got to stop this, Kathleen," she murmured between breaths. "You can't keep using this man to get off. He could be a criminal, for goodness' sake." It was a statement she knew probably wasn't true and one that hurt to consider seriously. Kathleen's heart and body ached for a man she couldn't be one hundred percent certain was innocent.

Kathleen took another shower, only this one was as cold as she could stand it. She was hoping to drown out the smoldering desires she was still experiencing for Morgan. After several minutes, Kathleen dried herself off, wrapped her body and hair in thick towels and sat on her bed. Kathleen knew she had to get her feelings under control and she needed advice on the best way to handle her situation with Morgan. She reached for her phone and called her sister. For the first time in her career, Kathleen was afraid that she was about to break a cardinal rule in investigation. A rule she'd always believed in and followed. It was the first thing her boss told her when she started: never get emotionally or physically involved with a target. Deep down inside, Kathleen knew she was about to do both.

Chapter 6

Kathleen set her phone on the nightstand while she changed back into her nightclothes. She was using her towel to squeeze the excess water from her hair when her video call connected. "Kathleen, why am I looking at one ugly-ass lamp?" Hannah asked.

"Oh sorry. Hold on a second." Kathleen pulled her hair up into a high ponytail and reached for the phone. She smiled at Hannah, a near mirror image of herself. "I was getting ready for bed."

"Bed?" Hannah checked her watch. "It's only nine."

"Yes, in California. I'm in Texas, remember, and it's eleven here."

"Oh yeah. I forgot."

"Where you going all dressed up? Not like you need much of a reason." Kathleen laughed.

"True, but tonight I have one. I'm going to the opening of a friend of mine's new restaurant."

"Oh…well I guess we can talk later," Kathleen replied, trying but failing to hide the disappointment in her voice.

"Oh no, you don't. I know that look. What's going on?"

"I don't want to keep you from your friends."

"Stop that." Hannah leered at her sister and sat down. "You know the rules. Family comes first. I got lots of friends but only two sisters. What's up?"

"Thanks, Hannah, and I'll be quick."

"Don't worry about it. What's going on?"

"I need your advice about something, but for you to help me, I have to share some things with you about my work."

"Okay." Hannah's eyes widened with surprise just as Kathleen expected.

Kathleen knew she had to keep the specifics of her investigations secret. However, Hannah had to know that she had developed feelings for someone and the situation around that person but not his identity, to know just how complicated things had gotten.

"I met this man…" Kathleen watched the small smile spread across Hannah's face as she searched for the right words. "He's the target of my investigation."

Hannah's smile disappeared. "What? Kathleen, you've been without a man for a long time, and the first one you fall for is a criminal?"

"Don't call him that. He's not a criminal." That was a conviction that had started taking root in her mind and heart the more time she spent with Morgan. The revelations about Mr. Silva didn't hurt, either.

"He can't be a Boy Scout, either, if you're investigating him. You've never been wrong about the targets you've gone after before. Don't let hormones screw up your professional success. Trust me when I say mixing business with pleasure doesn't work."

"This isn't about you, sister dear. Now can I finish?"

Hannah crossed her arms and pursed her lips. "This should be good."

Kathleen was having second thoughts about sharing the dilemma with her sister until she remembered Hannah's response was coming from a place of love and real concern. "Ever since I met this man I can't seem to stop thinking about him...dreaming about him."

"That's your hormones talking. Maybe it's just a bad boy phase you're going through. You'll get over it," Hannah concluded.

"It's not a bad boy phase, and I told you he's not a criminal. Morgan's strong...a man's man. He's extremely smart and family oriented. He reminds me of Dad."

"Then why are you investigating him?" She raised her left eyebrow.

Kathleen knew her sister's question was rhetorical, but she couldn't leave it out there in the universe like that, so she said, "All I can say is that a claim was brought against his company and not him personally."

"Remember what Dad always says?"

"We are our company," the two women chorused.

"Yes, Hannah but that's *our* company. I think this family is much like ours in that regard. There is no way his mother would do anything to hurt her company or their reputation."

Hannah frowned. "His mother?"

"Never mind that, what do I do?"

"About what?"

"These feelings..."

Hannah dropped her arms. "Do you think he's into you too?"

"I think so...maybe." Kathleen released an audible sigh. "I don't know."

"Well, if you're really into him, ask the man out."

"I thought about that, but I don't want to taint my investigation."

Hannah reached for her ringing phone. "Isn't it already tainted?" She sent the caller to voice mail. "You are having what I assume are sexy dreams about the man."

Yes, they are. "The dreams just started, and I pretty much have my answers regarding the investigation."

"Putting your hormones aside for minute. Can you honestly say with one-hundred-percent certainty that he is innocent of whatever it is you're investigating?"

"I'm ninety percent there."

"Then I recommend that you find that other ten percent before you do anything," Hannah stated.

"Looks like I'm about to get that chance tomorrow." She nodded in agreement.

"If you do, then bring him to Vista."

"Vista?"

"Yeah, that's the restaurant my friend is opening in Houston this weekend. It's their soft launch, so it won't be too crowded, no press and I'm his guest chef. That way I'll be able to check out the man who finally reminded my beautiful sister that she's a woman." Both women laughed. "But promise me one thing."

Kathleen was afraid to ask but replied, "What's that?"

"You won't do anything until you know for a fact that this man and his company are innocent of whatever it is that they are being accused of, okay? I know you, Kathleen. If you're wrong about him, you'll hate yourself."

Kathleen knew her sister was right and she couldn't put the lives of others in jeopardy because she was suddenly all hot and bothered for Morgan Kingsley. "I promise. I won't make a move until I'm one-hundred-percent sure."

"Good."

"But…"

"But what?" Hannah's phone rang again.

Kathleen rolled her eyes. "Please answer your hotline."

"Hold up." Hannah put the caller on Speaker. "Yes?"

"Hannah, where are you? Everyone's waiting," the frantic-sounding person on the line asked.

"I'll be there soon. Chill." Hannah ended the call.

"You should go, sis."

Hannah gave a nonchalant wave. "But what?"

Kathleen ran her right hand through her damp hair. "What if he says no or isn't interested in me?" she asked, her voice barely above a whisper. "You know I haven't dated in a while, so maybe I'm misreading the signals."

"I'm sure you're not. If he's not interested, then he's weak," Hannah stated matter-of-factly.

Kathleen burst out laughing, and before she knew it, she said, "Morgan Kingsley is most certainly not weak."

Hannah's eyes widened, and her whole face lit up like a kid discovering a favorite toy under the Christmas tree. "Morgan Kingsley? You want to do the nasty with Morgan Kingsley?"

Both hands flew to Kathleen's mouth. "Dammit!"

"Girl, you should've started with that. Morgan Kingsley is fine as hell, and you're right. I don't care what anyone says…they couldn't have done anything they're being accused of doing. The Kingsleys are good people."

"Wait, you know the Kingsleys?" A horrifying

thought popped into her mind. Had her sister and Morgan dated?

"Of course I know the Kingsleys. We all run in the same social circle. A circle you rarely visit."

Kathleen didn't want to ask, but she couldn't stop herself. "Have you and him ever…"

Hannah smiled. "You *really* do like him. No, we've never even met, not formally anyway. I wish you could have seen your face. If I'd said yes, you would have come after me through the phone," she replied, laughing.

Kathleen threw up her hands and shook her head. "Not funny, Hannah. Talking to you is like talking to a toddler sometimes." Hannah stuck out her tongue. "What does 'not formally' mean?"

"He's escorted his mother and her sister Elizabeth Kingsley to a few charity events that I've attended with Dad. You know, the ones you usually refuse to go to."

"Not this again. I don't refuse. It's just most of the events I'm asked about happen when I'm extremely busy with work, or they're halfway across the country."

"Which is why we have our very own planes, Kathleen."

"Cut me a break. I just went to one, remember?"

"Yes and only because it was about Mom," Hannah reminded her sister, her voice turning somber.

A sense of sadness seemed to hit them both at the same time. "Yeah, well, I was there," Kathleen murmured.

"We have some obligations that we as a family should address. We just need you to do better when it comes to your responsibilities to the foundation and all of us. Now I'm done. Okay?"

"Okay."

"Be careful with Morgan Kingsley."

"Why do you say that?" Kathleen frowned. She was nervous about what her sister was about to say.

"I hear he's not much for long-term commitments."

"Neither am I," Kathleen offered, knowing that was a lie. She'd never really been one to date. Her life had been centered on her work; she had no idea how she felt about commitments.

Hannah burst out laughing. "Seriously, Kathleen? You're no virgin, but you're not a serial dater either. All I'm saying is Morgan Kingsley is the type of man you play with...not marry."

"Why do you keep trying to marry me off? I told you, I'm not looking for a husband."

"Then what are you looking for...a one-off, a hit-and-run? Are you looking for Mr. Goodbar?"

Kathleen felt her whole face contort. "What?"

"A one-night stand...just sex."

Kathleen looked away from her sister for a moment before returning to glaring at Hannah. "Maybe. Maybe I want to sow a few wild oats myself."

Hannah gave her head a slow shake and picked up her purse. "You couldn't find an oat if you stood in the middle of an oat field."

Kathleen gave her sister the evil eye. "Go to your opening and thanks for the advice."

"Anytime. Be careful, and I love you."

"Love you more." Kathleen blew a kiss at the screen and disconnected the call.

Kathleen turned off the light and lay down on her bed. She thought about everything her sister said and realized she had no idea what she wanted from Morgan. The only thing Kathleen knew for sure was that everything about the man intrigued her and she was attracted to him in a way she'd never been with anyone else.

Kathleen had to find out why and what it meant. Was it just physical or might it go deeper than that? But first, Kathleen needed to see if the picture everyone painted about the Kingsleys was accurate, and she had to figure out how. As Kathleen closed her eyes, an idea started to take shape.

Chapter 7

The next morning Kathleen dressed in her favorite gray Vera Wang pantsuit. It showcased her curves and gave her an added level of confidence whenever she was a little nervous about the day's outcome. She paired it with a scoop-neck white blouse, offering only a hint of cleavage, and low-heeled gray shoes. Kathleen told herself that she was just changing up her wardrobe and dressing up had nothing to do with the fact that she was expecting Morgan to attend her eight o'clock class that day.

From the moment Kathleen arrived at the plant, she found herself staring at all the time-tracking devices in her wake. If it wasn't the watch she wore on her wrist to help track her steps, it was the large clock on the wall and every computer screen she passed in the Kingsley training center. They all read the same, sending her a clear message. It was ten forty-five in the morning, and Morgan was nowhere to be found.

Kathleen was using the small training room, which usually held fifty individuals; today there were only thirty people in attendance. Normally she'd have a packed house, but she was competing with another required policy training session down the hall. Kathleen had considered that Morgan might have forgotten he needed to be there instead of her safety training class, so she checked. After finding out that he wasn't there either but on the grounds, she deduced that he'd changed his mind and blown her off. Kathleen couldn't figure out what angered her the most, the fact that Morgan hadn't shown or that her disappointment was overpowering and purely personal.

"Five minutes, everyone. You should be wrapping up your test now," she announced to the class.

"I'm done. Easiest test ever," one of the trainees stated, his voice loud and full of pride.

Kathleen smiled. "We'll see in four minutes, won't we?"

Everyone laughed, then suddenly the room fell silent, and everyone's attention returned to their computers. Kathleen, standing with her back to the door, could feel the presence of someone behind her as the mood in the room shifted. She turned to find Morgan standing in the doorway wearing a pair of blue coveralls and work boots. While most of the men who worked in the plant wore the same uniform, it was something about the way he wore his. It fit his tall, fit body like a well-cut suit. Morgan took three steps into the room, and like a magnet, Kathleen was drawn toward him, matching his movement.

Kathleen's eyes roamed his body, and her mouth suddenly became dry as a desert, her mind going blank. Only one word snapped in her head and unfortunately escaped her lips before she could stop it. "Yummy." *Dammit.* Kathleen was thankful that the trainees couldn't hear her. Too bad Morgan did.

The corners of Morgan's mouth rose as he stared down at Kathleen. "What was that?"

Kathleen gave her head a quick shake, pushed her shoulders back and stared up at him. "May I help you, Mr. Kingsley?"

Morgan took another small step forward, ignoring a few of his onlooking staff. "You just might be able to, only now isn't the time or the place," he replied in a hushed tone.

Kathleen cleared her throat and bit the inside of her lip. "Is that so?"

Morgan nodded slowly. His eyes scanned his team, sending them an unspoken message to mind their own business. Kathleen folded her arms across her chest. "You're late. You promised you'd come." Kathleen knew she was sounding more like a disappointed girlfriend than a professional trainer, not to mention a top investigator for one of the government's most trusted and respected agencies, but for reasons she couldn't explain she just didn't care.

Morgan reached for Kathleen's hand, sending very familiar shockwaves throughout her body. He led her out into the hall, closing the door behind him. Morgan didn't release Kathleen's hand, and she didn't bother pulling herself free. "I apologize for not showing up. I should've sent someone to explain where I was. We had a situation in one of our tanks that needed my attention this morning and you can't make calls from inside the tanks. Whenever one of my people could be in danger, I need to be on-site."

"Oh... I understand." Kathleen had heard that Morgan would never ask anyone to do anything he was not willing to do himself and if something dangerous was happening, he was always lending a helping hand.

Morgan pulled Kathleen closer and intertwined their hands. "I didn't make you a promise. I made a statement that I hoped to be able to keep. For me a promise is personal, and I keep my promises, which is why I rarely make some."

Kathleen lowered her head, and a sense of disappointment was suddenly upon her, fighting the desire she had for the man who was openly holding her hands. Morgan freed his right hand, captured her chin with his thumb and index finger and raised her head. He gazed into her eyes and said, "The promises I make to you, Miss Winston, I plan to keep."

They stood staring into each other's eyes as Morgan ran his thumb slowly across her lips. It was like he was lighting a match. Kathleen knew the fire he'd ignited inside her could consume them both if she weren't careful. Needing to break the connection, Kathleen closed her eyes, pushed out a slow breath and took a small step backward.

Morgan was afraid he might have gone too far too fast. He knew he had to act. Now that he'd decided to pursue Kathleen there was no way he was giving up now. "Is it too late?"

"Too late for what?" she whispered.

"To join your training. Would you prefer to try again tomorrow morning?"

"No. It's not too late. In fact, you're right on time."

Morgan opened the door and gestured for Kathleen to enter. "After you."

"Thank you." Kathleen walked back into the room. "Excuse me, everyone. Now that you've finished with the sectional quiz, I assume you're all done and passed." She scanned the room for signs that anyone hadn't. Having found none, she continued. "Now I would like to move on to our next test."

Everyone moaned, and Morgan raised his hand. "Excuse me. There's a test? Do I need time to prepare?"

The room broke out into laughter. "It's not that type of test," Kathleen said, smiling up at Morgan, sending his heart and mind racing. Kathleen turned her attention to the rest of the class. "The new regulations require that you be able to put your protective gear on in less than two minutes during a level-three emergency."

"And we can," Morgan declared proudly. "Some of us can do it in under a minute."

"Really?"

"You doubt me?"

"As a matter of fact I do," she replied, winking at the class. "I think you'll need to prove it."

"Excuse me, Kathleen," one of the male trainees called out from the front row.

Morgan was irritated by the casual nature of how he addressed Kathleen. It seemed a little too personal. Morgan's eyes lasered in on the trainee. He walked over to the young man and read his badge. "Bloom, is it?"

"Yes, sir," he replied, sitting up in his chair.

"We haven't met yet. I'm Morgan Kingsley, and I'd prefer it if you were less casual when you address our guest."

"It's fine—"

"No, it's not. It's either Miss Winston or Miss Kathleen. It's more appropriate in this setting," he instructed.

"Yes, sir," the young man replied.

Morgan could feel Kathleen's eyes boring into his skin. He knew she didn't agree, but he didn't care. He didn't like the idea of anyone getting too personal with

Kathleen. Morgan turned toward her. "Shall we continue, Miss Winston?"

"We most certainly can. I need everyone to join me at my exhibit area." Kathleen walked over to a long cafeteria-style table positioned on the side of the room and covered by a red tablecloth. "As I was saying, you need to be able to change into all of this gear in two minutes or less."

"And like I said, with the exception of a few new people in the room, most of my men can."

Kathleen folded her arms at her breast. It was a move he loved and hated. "When was the last time you had a level-three crisis at this plant, Mr. Kingsley? You know, severe weather, explosions and fires."

"Yes, I know. Never, but we have monthly drills, so if it happens our brain will kick in, and thanks to the repetitiveness of our actions, we'll know just what to do," he stated confidently.

"Yes, the brain stores repetitive actions. However, that area of the brain is like any other muscle. If you don't use it on a regular basis, it can go limp when you need it the most." Kathleen heard gasps and snickers spread throughout the group and she instantly regretted her choice of words. She was hoping she wasn't turning as red as her tablecloth.

"Trust me—that would never happen," Morgan stated in a lowered tone.

Kathleen needed to bring the room back under control. She picked up a pair of glasses and headphones. "To ensure that it doesn't, you need to do your monthly drills under similar circumstances as a level-three emergency."

"And how do you suppose we make that happen?" Morgan asked.

"By using these." Kathleen held up the glasses and headphones for everyone to see. "The eyeglasses offer a blurred view, and the headphones will play the noises you'd expect to hear during such emergencies. While wearing these, you'll have to put all your emergency gear on in less than two minutes."

"Is that so?"

"Yes, it is. Does everybody understand?" Everyone nodded, except Morgan. "So who's first?"

The room went still, and all eyes landed on Morgan. "Looks like I'm it."

The room broke out in loud cheers and claps. "In under a minute," Kathleen reminded Morgan.

Morgan smiled. He turned his back to his staff and lowered his voice. "Once I get all that gear on, even with the distraction, in less than a minute, you'll allow me to take you to dinner." Morgan held her gaze as he waited for Kathleen's response.

Kathleen couldn't think rationally whenever he set his gorgeous eyes on her. "Fine. And if you don't, I'll take you out, and I get to pick the place," she replied, deciding to take her sister's advice.

Morgan offered Kathleen a brittle smile. He took the glasses and headphones out of her hand and went over to the table. "When do we start?" he asked, looking down at everything before him.

"Once you put the glasses and headphones on, I'll tap your shoulder, and you can begin." Kathleen held up a timer that was also on the desk. "We'll track your time with this. Ready whenever you are, Mr. Kingsley."

Morgan put the glasses on first. "Wow, I can't see a thing with these on. Everything's all fuzzy."

"Yes, I know. The glasses are designed to distort your vision the way smoke or excess water coming down on you might."

"Water?" one of the female trainees asked, touching her hair.

"Yes, from the heavy-duty sprinkler system the plant must have in place. Trust me, in such an emergency the last thing you'll be worried about is how your hair looks." Kathleen replied.

"Unless it's on fire," she rebutted.

"Which is why you'll be grateful to have those sprinklers functioning properly and ready to go… They are ready to go, right?" she asked, scanning the room for any tempered responses. Kathleen felt ridiculous for even asking the question, but she couldn't seem to turn off the investigator in her.

A number of different positive responses came flying at her. "Would you like to see the schematics?" Morgan asked.

"That won't be necessary."

"Let's get this show started," Morgan said, placing the headphones over his ears.

Kathleen tapped Morgan's shoulders and hit the start button on the timer. She stood back and watched as Morgan selected each piece of clothing and safety apparatus, slipping them onto his body as if he could see where each piece lay. It took him fifty-eight seconds to become fully dressed, having put each safety piece on in its appropriate order. The order in which things should be put on was a little tidbit she usually held back so she could see how much each person knew and understood. Once he finished, the room broke out in a loud cheer, and Morgan removed his glasses and headphones.

"Congratulations, Mr. Kingsley. That was quite impressive," she stated, surprised he was able to complete the task so quickly.

"Thank you," he said as he placed the glasses and headphones back on the table.

"I'll go next," Bloom offered, making his way to the table.

"Sure. Why doesn't everyone partner up? There are four sets of gear. One can dress while the other keeps time." Morgan had removed all his gear and was now standing close to the door.

"Going somewhere?" Kathleen asked, secretly hoping that he wasn't.

"Of course not. I'm here for the duration of the class. If you don't mind?"

"'Course not." Kathleen suddenly felt very warm and extremely happy.

"So how's Friday?"

Kathleen tried to hold back her broad smile but couldn't. "Friday's fine."

"And to show how good of a sport I am you can pick the restaurant. As long as there's meat."

Kathleen covered her mouth and laughed. "You're a carnivore. Why am I not surprised?"

Morgan smirked.

Chapter 8

Morgan sat back and watched as his team tried to complete the task in less than two minutes. Most were successful and for the few exceptions who struggled, Kathleen walked them through the process in such a way they got it on their second try. He was impressed with her approach and her extensive knowledge of not only the equipment but the proper order and manner in which it should be used. He was rethinking his position on her interactive approach, at least for this portion of their safety training.

He struggled to stay focused because no matter how hard Kathleen tried to downplay it, her gorgeousness was a distraction, to him anyway. Wearing little to no makeup only enhanced her natural beauty, and now he knew how soft her skin was too. The simple outfit she wore showed off how physically fit she was, and Morgan found himself wondering what she wore underneath it. Morgan had been with many women, but none of them affected him in such a way, especially at work. He knew he had to keep things professional while at the plant but staying away from Kathleen was no longer an option.

"Great job, everyone," Kathleen announced. "It's nearly lunchtime, so let's stop here. Thank you for the terrific work this morning. For those of you coming back this afternoon, I'll see you at one thirty sharp. Those who aren't—" her eyes jumped to Morgan "—thanks for your participation."

Morgan watched as his team filed out of the room one by one. "Wonderful job."

"Thank you." Kathleen packed up her things.

"Let me help with that." Morgan reached for the box on the floor at the same time as Kathleen, and his hand covered hers.

Kathleen released an audible gasp. Morgan dropped the box, took Kathleen's hand and pulled her into him. "You're the most beautiful woman I've ever seen."

"I doubt that, but thank you," she replied, her voice barely above a whisper.

Morgan ran his right hand slowly down the side of her face and stared into her eyes. "To me, beauty goes beyond how a person looks. It was a thing of beauty how you handled my team, especially the ones having difficulty meeting the task. It's beautiful to see how much you know and understand, not to mention how passionate you are about our business. Yes, I understand that as a trainer, it's your job, but your level of understanding comes from somewhere else, and I can't wait to find out where. Your physical beauty is gravy to the meat and potatoes of who you are."

Kathleen lowered her eyes. "That's very kind of you to say, considering…" She freed her hand, picked up the box and continued packing up her supplies.

"Considering the hard time I gave you when you first arrived."

"Yes. Not to mention the distance you kept."

Morgan helped her pack. "I had my reasons."

"Care to share?" The question was out of Kathleen's mouth before she could do anything about it.

Morgan's phone rang. He pulled it out, read the name and sent the caller to voice mail. "Not really but I will say this. I'm done avoiding you." He placed his hands in his pockets.

"So it wasn't my imagination?"

"No." Morgan's phone rang again.

Kathleen saw it was a woman's name that appeared. "Care to take that?" Kathleen had never been the jealous or possessive type, and Morgan didn't belong to her, so she didn't understand why all of a sudden she felt like taking his phone and throwing it against the wall.

"It can wait."

"You mean *she* can wait," she replied, giving him the side-eye as she placed the last of her supplies in the box. "Look, if you're seeing someone—"

"If I was seeing someone, I wouldn't have asked you out. I most certainly wouldn't be standing here, forcing myself to keep my hands in my pockets, so I won't keep touching you."

Thank goodness, and the feeling is mutual. But I have to know.

Kathleen turned and faced Morgan, placing her right hand on her hip. "We both know you have a bit of a reputation when it comes to women."

"We do?"

"Are you denying that you're a serial dater?" Kathleen asked, using her sister's words.

"A serial dater. That's an interesting analogy."

"Yes, but is it an accurate one?"

Morgan removed his hands from his pockets and crossed his arms at his chest. He leaned against the table. "If your definition of 'serial dater' is a single person who dates a number of women over a certain period of time, then I guess that would be accurate. But I only date one woman at a time."

"I appreciate your honesty."

"What about you?" he asked.

"What about me?" She scrunched up her face.

"Are you a serial dater too?"

Kathleen shook her head. "Hardly. *Serial* usually implies three or more. My two relationships wouldn't make the cut."

"I find that hard to believe. So you're more the relationship type," Morgan worked out.

"You make that sound like a bad thing."

"Not at all. I watched my brothers' lives change for the better, thanks to their wives."

"But that's not something you want for yourself."

"I just haven't been so lucky when it comes to relationships," he said, his face expressionless.

"I'm sure there's a story behind your lack of luck."

"What about your two relationships? Were they serious?"

Kathleen's phone rang. "One second."

"Saved by the bell."

Kathleen laughed as she moved over to the desk and picked up her cell phone. She saw that it was her father calling. "Excuse me for one moment."

"I'll step out," Morgan offered.

"No!" Their eyes collided, and Kathleen only hoped

she didn't look as desperate as she sounded. "I mean, you don't have to leave."

Morgan stood, poker-faced, and nodded.

Kathleen turned her back to Morgan and answered the call in French. "Hello, Dad, is everything okay?"

"Yes, can't a father just call and check on his children?"

"Of course you can, but I'm working, and you know that, so if everything's okay, you must have a reason for calling me in the middle of the afternoon."

"Well, I was hoping you'd come home for the weekend. I'll send your plane for you. It's just sitting in the hangar."

Kathleen would have loved to spend the weekend in New Orleans but she had a date with Morgan, and she wanted that just a little more. "I'd love to, Dad, but I have plans in Houston this weekend. I'll come home soon—I promise." Kathleen ended the call and turned to face Morgan. She was expecting to get hit with some questions regarding her bilingual status, only to her surprise he smiled and said, "So where's home?"

Kathleen blinked. "You speak French?"

"Only a few words here and there. I understand it more."

"Did you take a class in high school or college?" she questioned, smiling.

"Not exactly," he replied, offering her a knowing look and scratching his chin with his right thumb.

"Oh, an old girlfriend taught you."

"Something like that," he admitted, clenching his jaw.

Kathleen shifted her weight from one leg to the other. "I sense there's a story there."

"One for another time. So where's home? I gathered your dad wants to see you," he asked.

"New Orleans."

"So—"

The door opened. "Oh, sorry if I'm interrupting," Adrian announced as he entered the room.

Kathleen checked her watch. "Oh goodness, I lost track of time. You're not… I mean—"

"I'll get out of your way," Morgan said.

"No, I can come back?" Adrian offered.

"It's cool," he replied before turning his attention back to Kathleen. "We'll finish this conversation later."

"I look forward to it." As Kathleen stood and watched Morgan walk out the door, for some reason she felt like all the air left the room with him.

"Are you all right?" Adrian asked with a concerned look on his face. "You look like you're going to be sick."

Kathleen walked over to her desk, picked up an unopened bottle of water and cracked the seal. She took several unladylike gulps, trying to extinguish the thirst brought on by Morgan's mere presence.

"I'm fine. Let's get started. What did you need help with again?" Kathleen was embarrassed about her lack of professionalism. She'd forgotten about her meeting with Adrian, and now she didn't recall why he was there.

"You wanted to see me, remember?" He frowned, looking at her like he was about ready to call for help. "Are you sure you're all right?"

Kathleen's mind had been filled with thoughts of Morgan, and she completely forgot her plan: she'd decided she needed to find out once and for all if her initial instincts about Morgan and the Kingsleys were wrong, or had her judgment been clouded by desire? What better way than to try to gain additional insight about the family than from someone who knew them well? Someone who might feel comfortable enough to tell her the truth, no matter what that truth might be, since he'd come to see her as just another fellow employee.

"Yes, of course. Forgive me, my mind was elsewhere. Please have a seat." Kathleen directed Adrian to a chair in front of her desk.

"What's up?"

"You've worked for the Kingsleys for a while now, correct?" Kathleen sat in the chair next to him.

"That's right."

"From what I've heard and seen, this seems to be a pretty great place to work."

"It is," he said and offered a laid-back smile.

"I was just wondering why, after all the bad publicity and bogus charges brought against them were dropped, they would make such major management changes now?"

Adrian shrugged. "I guess Ms. Victoria decided the time had come to step aside and let Alexander take over. She'd been training him for the role for years."

"Morgan's cousin…what's her name?"

"Kristen Kingsley."

"Yes, she stepped into Alexander's former role. I know she was VP of Operations but we're talking about a high profile COO position. No offense but she's a bit of a party girl according to social media. I would have thought others with less of a media presence would be more qualified for the role although Morgan would have been the next and best logical choice in my opinion." Kathleen only hoped Adrian thought she was advocating for Morgan versus investigating the choice.

The lazy smile he gifted her with told Kathleen he

was going down the path she led him to. "You don't need to worry about Morgan. He loves the role he plays. As for Kristen, yeah, she likes to party, but she too was trained for her role. Like her aunt Victoria, Kristen is smart and tough as nails. That's one bad bitch. Excuse my French. I mean that in a good way."

I hate that saying. That's not French. "It's fine."

"One thing about the Kingsleys—birthright only gets you the option of being first. You have to earn roles just like everyone else."

"Really? Most wealthy families with businesses expect their kids to be part of said business." *Mine most certainly did and Dad and my siblings remind me of that fact all the time.*

"True, and the Kingsleys are no different. However no one's forced to join the company and Victoria would never let nepotism ruin her bottom line," he said, laughing.

"I believe that." Kathleen was coming to realize she'd been wrong about the Kingsleys.

"Are you thinking about trying to come to work here full-time? I know we could use a smart trainer like you on staff. I can put in a good word for you with Morgan, if you like," he offered, seeming excited by the idea.

"Thanks, but that won't be necessary."

Adrian rose from his chair. "I'd better get back to work, unless you need something else."

"No, I'm good. Thanks for the information."

"Anytime. You really should think about my offer," Adrian reminded before walking out the door.

Kathleen touched her cheek where Morgan had caressed her skin. "I'm thinking about a lot of things."

Chapter 9

The next few days came and went with little interaction between Morgan and Kathleen. While Morgan was no longer avoiding her, he'd make sure when they did spend time together others were around. Morgan had never wanted a woman the way he found himself wanting Kathleen. Not even the woman he'd once planned to marry. There was just something about Kathleen that both enticed him and scared the hell out of him too.

It was Friday, and Morgan found himself watching the clock. He was excited about the fact that he'd soon have Kathleen alone and all to himself. The hours seemed to be moving slower than normal. Morgan was sitting at a table in the back of the cafeteria, watching his team members interact with each other when Kathleen approached him holding a tray with one of Ms. Monica's famous chef's salads and a bottle of water on it.

"May I join you?" Kathleen asked, smiling down at him.

Morgan stood, and his heart sped up. "Please."

Kathleen took a seat. "Thank you. You're not eating?"

Morgan sat down. "I had something earlier. How's your day going?" His cell phone rang and he sent the caller to his voice mail.

"Good. In fact, I'm done with my last class, so I thought I'd cut out early, if that's okay with you. My older sister has a few things she needs my help with this weekend."

Morgan puckered his brow. "Sure... No problem." *There goes our date.* They hadn't talked about it since Monday, so Morgan assumed Kathleen had either forgotten about it or changed her mind. Either way, he felt like a fool and had a sense of disappointment unlike anything he'd ever known.

Suddenly, he was drowning in it and had to get away from Kathleen before he said or did something that would embarrass them both. Morgan picked up his ringing phone. "Excuse me. I should take this. Have a good weekend, Kathleen." Morgan stood and made his way to the nearest exit. He had to use every bit of pride he had not to turn around and demand an explanation and try to change Kathleen's mind.

Kathleen watched Morgan disappear through the door before she could find out what the hell had just happened. She thought they'd reached a turning point. He was no longer avoiding her, and he'd sat in on several of her classes. He told her he was just auditing her work, but she knew there was more to it than that, and she loved it. She even caught him staring at her from across the room a few times. Now this... He just blew off their date. Kathleen was no longer hungry, but before she could dispose of her tray, she saw Ms. Monica and her assistant heading right for her table. They'd never officially met, but she certainly knew who she was.

"How's the salad, baby girl?" Ms. Monica asked.

"It's great," Kathleen replied, forcing a smile.

"Really? How would you know since you haven't touched it?"

"I mean, I'm sure it's great. It's just my stomach is a little upset all of a sudden," Kathleen explained, hoping it would appease the woman. It didn't.

"Roughage is what you need, then. It'll get things moving. Excuse my manners. I'm Monica, and this is my sous chef, Lori."

"Pleased to meet you," Lori replied, offering her hand, which Kathleen shook.

"I've been cutting onions so I won't shake your hand, but I will bump your elbow," said Monica. "You can call us Ms. Monica and Ms. Lori. Yes, I went to culinary school, but I never liked being called chef."

"Me either," Lori agreed.

"The titles go along with these fancy new uniforms." Ms. Monica looked down at the black pants and double-breasted black coat and pointed out the personalized embroidery. "They even got our names and titles on them. Rich people, I swear."

Lori laughed. "You should try putting something in your stomach. It might make you feel better."

Kathleen appreciated the concern and suggestion but she knew only one thing could make her feel better and he'd just left. "Thanks, but I'll be fine."

Ms. Monica placed her right hand on her hip. "A little stomachache isn't all that's wrong with you."

Kathleen could feel her emotions rising. Soon her face would flush, and she'd be fighting back tears. She had to bring herself back under control, and she needed a distraction. She picked up her fork and took several bites of her food. "This is good," she complimented through bites.

"I'm glad you like it, but I know something's up." Ms. Monica and Lori took seats across from Kathleen. "Care to talk about it?"

At times like these, even after seven years, she missed her mother very much. Irene Winston had been very easy to talk to, and Kathleen knew she'd know just how to make her feel better. Although Irene would never tell her what to do, she always informed Kathleen and her siblings that people were the sum of their decisions and while others might offer advice, ultimately, it was up to the individual to make the right choices for himself or herself.

"I'm fine… Really."

"Mm-hmm. Lori, you believe this child?"

Lori folded her arms across her ample breast. "Not at all."

"I bet Morgan said something he shouldn't have," Ms. Monica guessed.

Kathleen could feel her expression close up. "Not at all. Everything's—"

"Fine?" Ms. Monica supplied. "Child, I've known that boy most of his life, and I know the effect he can have on women."

"I've seen you too," Lori added, shaking her head.

"I've watched him watching you these last few days. There is an intense interest there, which means only two things."

Kathleen couldn't help but ask, "What's that?"

Ms. Monica held up her index finger. "One, he's feeling you. Isn't that what the kids call it?"

Kathleen laughed. "Yes, ma'am."

"And two—" another finger went up "—he's feeling you."

Kathleen presented a shy smile. "I—"

"Let me finish. Morgan's not like his brothers or his mother. He's a man of few words. With Morgan, actions speak louder. He doesn't like drama. Morgan tends to avoid things, leave things unsaid, which can cause problems."

"He has issues with communicating unless it's about work," Lori added.

"He's dated other women," Kathleen murmured, speaking without thinking. Fearing she'd said too much she quickly added, "Not that we're—"

"Child, please." Ms. Monica gave Kathleen a knowing look. "A blind man can see something is going on between you two. If he's gone all quiet on you or shut down, you'll have to make him tell you what's going on."

"That is, if you want him. If not, there's plenty in this town and elsewhere that do. Hell, if I was twenty years younger and a few pounds smaller..." Lori smiled and winked.

"You'd still be too old," Ms. Monica said, giving Lori the evil eye. She reached for Kathleen's hand. "Morgan's a good man. He just protects that heart of his. It has been broken once, and he's afraid to take a chance on letting it happen again."

"Really, when? Who was she? What happened?" Kathleen was spitting out questions like rapid fire. This new information took her completely by surprise, and she didn't know how she felt about knowing that Morgan once loved someone so much that he became afraid to let anyone else get close. Loving someone else like that again was something she didn't think he would be willing to do. Kathleen had never experienced that type of love before, and she was jealous of whoever this mystery woman was, the one who'd managed to steal Morgan's heart.

"That's not my story to tell. You should ask Morgan about it yourself unless, like you said, you two aren't dating." Ms. Monica rose from her seat, as did Lori. She reached for Kathleen's plate. "I'll go wrap this up. You can take it to go. I'll be right back."

"Thank you." Kathleen's eyes jumped between the two older women.

Kathleen sat back and waited for the wise women to return. She let Ms. Monica's words take hold as Kathleen recalled her sister's advice to make sure she was positive about Morgan before she did anything. *He doesn't want to get close to anyone.* Maybe he felt things were getting too close already. She certainly did.

That's why he blew off our date. Kathleen's heart dropped like she was riding on a roller coaster. She hated the idea that some mystery woman from Morgan's past was preventing them from finding out if what they were experiencing was real. She understood how ghosts from the past could stop her from pursuing things and people that might be good for her. She knew she'd been doing that most of her adult life, focusing solely on her career, driven in part by a need to avenge her mother's death, something she knew wasn't rational, but until now there hadn't been anything she'd wanted enough to make her think twice about her choices.

But her attraction to Morgan was proof that she needed more in her life than just work. He needed to improve his communication skills a bit. She was still very annoyed about the way he'd handled the situation.

Plus, his heartbreak had been a while ago. Maybe he had some other reason for not keeping their date.

Regardless, Kathleen had to tell him the real reason behind her visit before she left town. Now that she could officially clear them he deserved the truth, especially since her boss could confirm that Mr. Silva's concerns were misguided but there was no malicious intent.

Kathleen stood when she saw Ms. Monica approaching. "Here you go, my dear." She handed Kathleen a to-go box.

"Thank you…for everything."

Ms. Monica gave a nonchalant wave. "No problem. If you want to talk to Morgan, he's in Adrian's office right now."

"How do you know that?"

"Because I called to find out," Ms. Monica said, frowning like Kathleen's question was a waste of oxygen. "You two should talk. You might be surprised by the outcome."

Kathleen hugged Ms. Monica and walked out the door. It was time to end her stay at Kingsley. She'd done what she'd come to do. The charges were unsubstantiated, so it was time to go. Kathleen could send someone else to complete the rest of the training, as well as help with incorporating new regulations into their policy. Kathleen fought back tears. She couldn't comprehend continuing to work side-by-side with Morgan, knowing how much she wanted him…cared for him.

It was time to get her mind off Morgan and find some real bad guys to chase. The case of Kingsley Oil and Gas versus OSHA was now closed, and so, it seemed, was the budding love affair between her and Morgan Kingsley, and it was breaking her heart.

* * *

"So does everyone agree with the final sale price?" Alexander asked. A ripple of yeses came through the phone, but Morgan's mind was on the woman who'd just blown him off and not a piece of property their mother wanted.

"Morgan… Morgan, you still there?" Alexander asked. Morgan, who had been standing and staring out the window, turned and sat down behind the desk. "I'm here, and I'm fine with it too."

"Good—"

"Wait, you did say that included the mineral rights, correct?" Morgan asked.

"Yes, of course," Alexander replied.

"Are you okay?" Kristen Kingsley, the company's newly appointed COO, questioned, her concern coming through loud and clear.

"Yes, I'm fine. Just a bit distracted," Morgan replied.

"Anything you want to share?" Alexander asked.

Not in the least bit. The last thing he needed was for his family to know that the one woman he wanted didn't want him back. "No, I'm good."

The office door opened and an angry Kathleen walked in and slammed the door behind her. She was holding what looked like a to-go container. "The next time you want to blow off a woman for a date, you should at least have the decency to tell her."

Chapter 10

Morgan slowly rose from his seat. "Excuse me." He came from around his desk.

Kathleen placed her food container on the corner of his desk and stood defiantly in front of him. "At first I was going to let it go…exit gracefully. But you asked me out, then what…you changed your mind or did you just get a better offer?"

Morgan was confused, but by the scowl on Kathleen's face he knew she believed what she was saying. "I have—"

"And another thing, mister." She used her right index finger and poked him in the chest. "You don't say all those beautiful things to a woman and just kick her to the curb without an explanation. What, are we back in high school?"

Morgan grabbed her finger and held it at his heart. "I didn't kick you to the curb, and I certainly didn't blow you off. You said you were leaving early and doing something with your sister this weekend. I'd say *you* blew me off."

"No, I didn't." Kathleen stepped forward, closing the gap between them. "I wouldn't."

Morgan watched as Kathleen's expression morphed from angry to confused to desirous. He could see how sincere she was and he was overwhelmed with emotions. Morgan lowered his head, scanning Kathleen's face for any sign of rejection. Seeing none, he gently kissed her on the lips. Kathleen slid her hands up and around his neck, pressed her body against him and moaned his name in his mouth. Morgan deepened the kiss. Soon he heard, "Hello… Morgan."

Morgan broke off the kiss and looked over at the phone. "Dammit!"

"What's wrong?" Kathleen asked before she heard the laughing. "What was that?" Kathleen looked around the room.

"I was on a conference call when you came in."

Kathleen buried her face in his chest. "Oh no. I'm sorry," she replied.

"I'm not. It's okay. Chill, you guys," he ordered, his voice taking on a husky tone.

"I'll go," she whispered.

"Oh no, you don't. I'm not dealing with that crew by myself," Morgan said, snaking his arms around her waist.

"Who?"

"My family. Alexander, Brice and Kristen, I'd like to introduce you all to Kathleen Winston. Kathleen, the laughter coming through the phone is from two of my brothers and my cousin."

"Hi, everyone," Kathleen reluctantly replied, and everyone responded with an array of hellos.

Morgan bid farewell and ended the call. "Sorry about that. So…"

"So… What?" Kathleen asked, gifting him with a sexy smile.

Morgan captured a loose strand of hair and placed it behind her ear. "Can I have the pleasure of your company for dinner tonight?"

Kathleen smiled. "Yes."

"Where are we going?"

"I don't know yet. I haven't heard from that sister."

Morgan tilted his head. "That sister? How many sisters do you have?"

"Two, and one brother."

Morgan tightened his hold on Kathleen. "I don't care where we go. I just want to be with you."

Kathleen rose up on her toes and collapsed her hands around his neck. "I want to be with you too," she replied before kissing him passionately on the lips.

After finally coming up for air, Morgan asked, "Where do I pick you up?"

Kathleen stepped out of Morgan's hold, and he missed her instantly. She reached for his cell phone that sat in its dock on the desk and handed it to him. "Pull up my contact information, and I'll add my address."

Morgan did as she asked and handed his phone to her. After inputting her address, she said, "I live in Houston. I'll text you the time and location once I know the information."

Morgan looked down at his phone. "This zip code looks familiar. Do you live near Hermann Park?"

"Yes, my house isn't far from the park at all. I live in the North MacGregor Way area."

"Nice. That area has a lot of newly renovated homes."

"Yes, they do. I should go." Kathleen picked up her lunch container and walked toward the door. She looked over her shoulder and said, "I'll see you later."

Morgan gave a quick nod but kept his feet planted. He knew if he didn't he'd reach for Kathleen again and wouldn't be able to let her go. Morgan had never felt like this before, and while the power this woman suddenly had over him scared the hell out of him, he couldn't wait to explore where it would lead. Morgan turned his back to the door and picked up a stack of documents he had to review, knowing how difficult a feat that would be. He was having a hard time concentrating on anything except Kathleen, but had to give it a shot.

When Morgan heard his door open again, his heart started beating so hard, he just knew she would hear it. He grinned. "Forget something, Kathleen?"

"No, but apparently you did," Adrian stated as he entered the office.

Morgan checked his watch. "Oh man. You're right. I forgot all about the meeting."

"No worries, I stalled. Van is taking them on a quick tour of the plant. We have a few minutes." Morgan was sitting in his chair so Adrian took a seat in one of the chairs in front of the desk. "I assume this lack of memory has something to do with Kathleen."

The corners of Morgan's mouth turned up. *It has everything to do with her.* Morgan knew he couldn't admit that to Adrian because he would never hear the end of it. "Where are we meeting the Ultra Tech executives?"

"Ignoring the question only means that I'm right. That's cool. They're in the executive conference room back at the administration building," Adrian informed him, leering at his friend.

Morgan's smile widened. He knew there was a chance he'd get another glimpse at Kathleen before she left for the day. "Oh man, you got it bad," Adrian concluded as he stood and walked toward the door. "I know my office is pretty cool but you do know that you have an office somewhere down the hall."

"Technically the whole plant is my office," Morgan countered.

"In that case why don't you set up an office next to the training room," he said, laughing as he walked out the door.

"That's not a bad idea," Morgan murmured to himself.

After spending a few hours with her eldest sister, Kennedy, Kathleen had finally made it home. Hannah had given her the information for the restaurant, and she texted it to Morgan. His reply, See you soon, baby, had her feeling all warm and fuzzy inside, something she'd never felt before.

Between her work and hobby of collecting unique antiques, Kathleen never seemed to have the time, energy or desire to date. She stood in her exceptionally large walk-in closet—which was a dressing room much like her sister's—trying to determine what to wear when her doorbell rang. "Who could that be?" She made her way down the stairs. Kathleen knew Morgan wouldn't dare show up three hours early, especially after she told him to be there at eight thirty. After checking her security screen, she heaved a sigh, but, deep down she was happy to see her guest.

Kathleen opened the door. "Hello, Lisa. Hannah sent you," she stated.

"Yes. Hannah thought you might need a little help getting ready for your date."

Kathleen waved Lisa inside. "Sadly, she's correct. Wait, please tell me you were already in town."

"I was," she said, laughing.

"Good, follow me."

The two women climbed the stairs and returned to Kathleen's closet. "See the problem?" Kathleen pointed to her wardrobe.

The luxurious dressing room with a designer closet system would make anyone swoon.

Kathleen nodded and walked over to each compartment where her clothes were held and opened the doors.

"May I?" Lisa asked.

"Please."

Lisa walked up to each compartment and flipped through all the garments. Nearly everything had a designer label, but it was all conservative professional business attire. Only one compartment had what could be perceived as business casual clothes.

"Is that it?" Lisa frowned.

Kathleen shrugged and nodded. "Except my jeans, leggings and casual tops, that's it."

"I see why Hannah did what she did."

Kathleen exhaled noisily. "What did Hannah do?"

The doorbell rang, and Lisa smiled. "Right on time."

"Shall I get that?" Lisa asked with a gummy smile.

Kathleen dropped down on one of the two gray-and-white chaise longues in the closet. "Might as well." Kathleen knew her sister must've made arrangements for her to have something more appropriate to wear tonight. While she wanted to strangle her, Kathleen also wanted to thank Hannah. She only hoped there would be something she could wear that didn't scream *jump my bones*, in spite of the fact that was exactly what her wayward body wanted.

"Here we are," Lisa announced, returning to the closet. She held up two large stuffed garment bags that she hung on a freestanding rack. Lisa unzipped one, removed the clothes and hung them on the rack. She removed a small gift bag that she set on the dresser. Kathleen walked over to the rack, flipped through everything her sister sent and was pleasantly surprised. Everything suited her perfectly. All the outfits selected were sexy but not over-the-top, like those Hannah usually preferred, especially when she was going out.

"Wow, these are great. I can't believe she picked these out," Kathleen replied.

"She didn't," Lisa said, unpacking her makeup bag. "She sent me shopping for you. I've gotten a sense of what you like based on the few times I've had the pleasure of working with you."

"You most certainly did. Thank you. Now, how many do I get to pick and when do they go back?"

"You aren't some frumpy stepsister and we're certainly not your fairy godmothers. They don't go back."

"What?"

"Hannah bought them all. She figured this would be the first of many dates you'll be going on."

"There's, what, twenty outfits here?" Kathleen couldn't hold back her surprise.

"There're twenty-four actually," Lisa corrected.

Kathleen fought back tears. She knew Hannah always had her back and doing something like this was right up her alley, but it still touched her heart knowing that her sister always seemed to know when she needed her the most.

Lisa looked over Kathleen, who had her hair in a messy ponytail; she was wearing leggings and a long white T-shirt. She shook her head and said, "We better get started. We only have two and a half hours before Prince Charming arrives."

Kathleen giggled like a little girl. "He most certainly is that."

"But first." Lisa picked up the small gift bag she'd placed on the dresser and handed it to Kathleen. "This is from both of us."

Kathleen's brows drew together. "What's this?"

"Something we both hope you'll need, if not tonight, then very soon."

Kathleen pulled out the decorative tissue paper and looked inside the bag. Her mouth fell open and her heart raced at the idea of using their gift. She bit her bottom lip and smiled. "Thank you," she whispered.

Chapter 11

Morgan admired all the different style homes he passed as he made his way to Kathleen's house. North MacGregor Way community was well-known for its historic and eclectic homes near downtown Houston. Morgan pulled his silver Aston Martin—a passion for expensive cars was the one indulgence all the Kingsleys shared—into Kathleen's circular driveway, which sat on a corner lot in a tree-lined area. Morgan grabbed the bottle of Domaine Ramonet Montrachet Grand wine on the front seat and exited the car.

He stood back and admired the single-family home and its large wooden door with a stained-glass center. Morgan rang the bell and nervously waited for Kathleen to answer. When the door opened, Morgan stood speechless as his eyes took their fill of the ravishing creature before him.

For three weeks Morgan had had the pleasure of getting to know the brilliant and charming woman who tried to downplay her beauty. Kathleen never even wore jewelry at work. However, the radiant woman standing before him, wearing a formfitting black wrap dress, high heels and had her hair held up with a black crystal clip, was a sight to behold. Teardrop diamond earrings were the perfect elegant accessories to the outfit.

"Good evening, Morgan," Kathleen greeted him with a broad smile.

Note to self: she likes diamond earrings. Get it together, man. "Good evening. This is for you," he said, offering her the bottle of wine.

"Thank you. Please come in." Kathleen stepped aside and allowed Morgan to enter. Kathleen read the bottle's label. "Very nice, and it happens to be one of my favorites."

"Really?"

"Yes, my sister Hannah is a chef and insists on nothing but the best and she introduces me to a lot of really cool things."

"Good. My cousin Kristen recommended it," he confessed.

"You're not much of a wine person," she guessed, laughing.

"Not really. I mean, a glass or two at dinner is fine, but it's not my go-to choice when I want to sit back and chill."

"Let me guess. You're more of a beer-and-whiskey guy," she said, leading him out of her foyer.

"That I am," he confirmed. They walked into the open living area, and Morgan was taken aback by how nicely she'd infused a contemporary style that didn't diminish the historical feel of the house.

"You have a beautiful home."

"Thank you. Let's take this into the kitchen. This way."

Morgan's heart nearly stopped when Kathleen turned and offered him a view of her perfectly round behind.

He commanded his body, which was starting to stir, to behave. "When was it built?"

"In 1940. It came up on auction, and I bought it. Renovated it myself," Kathleen announced proudly.

"You renovated it?" He raised his eyebrows.

Kathleen stopped in her tracks and turned to face him. "I most certainly did. Yes, I had help, but I designed it, picked the materials and you see these wood floors?" She pointed down. "I refurbished them myself. In fact, I did all the flooring throughout the house myself, including the tiling."

"Seriously?"

"Just me with these." She placed the wine bottle under her arm and presented him her hands. "My own two hands."

"Wow. I'm impressed."

Kathleen smirked. "Don't be. It's kind of in my genes."

"What does that mean?"

"My family's into construction, and I picked up a thing or two. Along with my love of antiquing, renovating turned into a hobby," she explained.

"That's some hobby."

"I guess…" Kathleen led him through an open set of French doors that took them into the dining area and to a gray-and-white, gourmet-style kitchen. The large marble island with seating for six offered in-kitchen dining. There was plenty of storage and modern appliances, except for the old-fashioned six-burner yellow stove and oven.

"Damn, Kathleen, this kitchen is something else. Where did you find that stove?"

"I didn't. My sister Hannah is a chef, remember."

"Okay?" He frowned, not sure what that meant.

"Well, she found it for me." Morgan nodded while he gave the stove a closer look. "She cooks for me from time to time, so she insisted that I have a stylish and quality stove for her to use."

Morgan laughed. "She sounds like my mother and cousin Kristen. They're all about quality and style."

Kathleen had all but closed the case against Kingsley Oil and Gas, yet she was still curious about the reason behind the recent change in leadership. She figured now was the best time to ask about Kristen and Alexander's promotions, get it straight from the horse's mouth, so to speak. "We have a few minutes before we have to go. Can I get you anything?"

"No, I'm good."

Kathleen placed the bottle in the refrigerator. "Do you mind if I ask you about something?"

"Of course not."

"You mentioned your cousin Kristen…" Kathleen bit the inside of her lip.

"Yeah, what about her?"

"I know she has just been promoted to COO for your company, and please don't take offense to this, but she doesn't seem like the obvious choice." She presented a small smile.

"Obvious to whom? Those idiots out there who think she got the job just because she's a Kingsley?" His jaw clenched. "Or maybe those assholes in our social circle who think just because she's had a few episodes in her personal life splattered all over social media that she's not serious enough to get the job done. Or could it be our competitors, who are trying to taint her reputation? They are the same ones who've gone up against us and know she's a brilliant businesswoman who's been trained by the best and is the perfect person to help my brother run our company and take us to the next level."

Morgan's mood had changed, and Kathleen wanted to kick herself for even bringing it up. His passion for his family and their company rivaled that of her own family, something she lacked and was coming to realize had been a disservice to herself. "I didn't mean to upset you."

"*You* didn't. Some people think that, because we're a privately held company and can manage things the way we wish, we'd overlook quality people for roles in favor of a family member. Victoria Kingsley would never do such a thing. Now, have we all been groomed to join our family's business? We most certainly have, and we've been trained from the ground up in fact. But if we weren't up to the task we wouldn't be given the opportunity to destroy something our parents spent their lives building just because we're family. My mother's not built that way. In fact, my brother Brice nearly got fired for letting his personal life interfere with business. Plus, not all the Kingsleys are in the business."

"Yes, your mother's one intense woman," she said, leading him back into the living room.

"You have no idea."

She did. Victoria Kingsley had a well-earned reputation for being a hard-ass when it came to her business, dealing with the regulatory branches of the government and being very protective when it came to her family. Facts she knew from her investigative role at OSHA that she wasn't ready to share with Morgan just yet.

Kathleen reached for her clutch purse that sat on the antique table behind the sofa. "Did you not want the job?"

"Hell, no. I hate wearing suits, let alone dealing with them all the time."

Kathleen admired the expensive, well-tailored black Giovanni suit and black collarless shirt he was wearing. "You certainly look great in them," she complimented.

"Thank you, and I believe I failed to mention how breathtakingly beautiful you look tonight."

Morgan's words and the way he was looking at her sent warm tingles to the lower half of her body. Kathleen knew her face was probably as red as the bottoms of her expensive shoes. "Thank you. Shall we go?"

"After you." Morgan gestured with his hand for her to lead the way.

Kathleen set her house alarm and walked out the door. She felt Morgan's eyes on her before the warmth of his hand was placed on the small of her back. Kathleen inhaled quickly. Morgan opened the car door and helped her inside. "Thank you," she said, her voice barely above a whisper. Kathleen cleared her throat as she watched him walk around the car. His model good looks, alpha male demeanor and sweet nature made Kathleen want him even more.

Morgan got into the driver's side. "So where are we headed?"

"There's a place in the Museum District called Vista." She opened her purse and pulled out a small piece of paper with an address written on it and handed it to him." *Hannah better be on her best behavior.*

"I know where this is. There used to be a bar in that spot," he informed, pulling out of the driveway.

"I wouldn't know. I don't go out much."

"Why is that?" he asked, making his way out of her neighborhood and onto the highway. "You can't expect me to believe men aren't lining up to take you out. I'm sure a few of mine are asking you out, in fact.

Kathleen saw Morgan's hands grip the steering wheel and the muscle in his jaw twitched. His eyes glanced over at her before returning to the road. Kathleen liked the idea that the thought of her going out with someone else annoyed him. She wished she'd worn her hair down so she'd at least have some cover when her cheeks started to warm from the embarrassment.

"Well…"

"Yes, I get asked out—"

"By my men," he finished.

"A couple, but I haven't dated anyone since college." There was a slight tremor in her voice that she couldn't hide.

Morgan tightened his grip on the steering wheel as she fell silent. He pulled into a vacant lot and Kathleen could see they were just down the street from the restaurant. Morgan turned off the engine and angled his body toward her. "Did something happen to you in college?" he asked, his tone hard.

Kathleen watched the emotions on Morgan's face morph from shock to anger, and his eyes narrowed. For several seconds Kathleen wasn't sure what he might be thinking. Then it finally dawned on her. Women on college campuses were being sexually assaulted every day. Kathleen reached for his forearm and squeezed it.

"Oh no, nothing bad happened to me. I promise." Kathleen could almost see the anxiety leaving his body. Morgan had no idea who she really was. If he did, he would have known about the security team that attended school, including their Ivy League colleges, with all the Winston girls. Their security's presence and antics on campus had made several media outlets' coverage.

"After my mom died all I wanted to do was focus on my career. I had a new purpose in life and relationships never fit into my plans," she explained.

Morgan tilted his head. "And now?"

"Now—" Kathleen captured his hand and intertwined their fingers "—I guess we'll see."

He brought her hand to his lips and kissed the back of it. "Yes, we will."

When he thought Kathleen might have experienced sexual harassment in college, Morgan's mind flashed back to what that bastard Perez had tried to do to both his aunt and sister-in-law. Morgan figured she might not have been able to fight off some bully trying to take advantage of her had she not had the financial means to exact vengeance the way his mother had when Perez attacked her sister.

"When my father and uncle died over twenty years ago, our lives changed significantly," he said.

"I can imagine and relate." Kathleen rubbed the top of her hand over his.

"We all handled our grief differently, but my aunt Elizabeth took it exceptionally hard, as you'd imagine. She went away for a while."

"What do you mean, she went away?"

His mouth set in a hard line. "Aunt Elizabeth had a bit of a breakdown. When she started getting back to her old self again, she would go out and see people. You know, in social settings."

Kathleen nodded her understanding but remained quiet.

"Well, one of those people was Perez—"

"The man who tried to ruin your company."

"Yes. Perez attacked my aunt…tried to…" Morgan

focused on the warmth of Kathleen's touch to help him stay in control.

Kathleen squeezed his hand. "Tried, so he didn't hurt her, right?"

"No."

"Thank God."

Morgan nodded. "By the sad look that transformed your beautiful face, the change in your voice and the way you avoided looking at me, I assumed the worst. I thought someone—"

"No one did anything—I'm fine." Kathleen brought Morgan's hand to her mouth and kissed his palm. "Let's go have dinner."

Morgan started the car and pulled onto the street, steering with one hand while keeping a strong grip on Kathleen's with the other. The idea that anyone would try to hurt any innocent person, especially a woman, made Morgan crazy. His heart was racing as he drove. Morgan ran his thumb across hers, and Kathleen squeezed his hand. His heart began to slow its rapid pace. It was as if she was sending him a message that she was fine. Morgan could feel her eyes on him, and when he glanced over at her, she gifted him with a relaxed smile. In that moment, he swore to himself that no one would ever hurt his woman…including him.

Chapter 12

Kathleen was surprised by the lack of fanfare typical of Hannah's events. Morgan pulled into the front of the restaurant and waved off the approaching valet. Exiting the car, he came around and opened Kathleen's door, then he helped her out and held her hand. Morgan gave the key to the valet along with two one-hundred-dollar bills and said, "Keep it close." That shouldn't have been an issue since he noticed all the up-close spots for valet cars were empty.

"Yes, sir," the young man replied, his eyes roaming between the money in his hands and the expensive car he was about to drive.

There were two big floodlights outside lighting the way, a red carpet had been rolled out and several valets were waiting at the ready, yet no one was around. "Are you sure this is the right spot?" Morgan asked Kathleen.

Kathleen, who looked just as confused as he felt, said, "I'm sure. This is the address my sister sent me."

"Well, for a grand opening, they're not getting much business. The owners should fire their PR agency," Morgan joked.

They both laughed. "Yes, they should."

Morgan led Kathleen inside, and a pretty blonde woman greeted them with a big smile on her face. She was obviously the hostess. The woman was wearing a short black dress and high strappy heels, a look obviously meant to grab the attention of the male customers. While she certainly would meet her goal with other men, Kathleen noticed that Morgan didn't seem fazed by the woman.

"Welcome to Vista," she announced, directing her attention to Morgan.

"Thank you," Kathleen replied as Morgan gave a quick nod. "I'm Kathleen Winston, and we have a reservation."

"Yes, ma'am. We've been expecting you. Please follow me."

"We've," Morgan whispered in Kathleen's ear.

Kathleen shrugged and did as she was asked. The young woman led them into a room that was dimly lit in spite of the many chandeliers that hung from the wooden ceiling. Slate tiles covered the floors and a ceiling-to-floor glass bar ran along one wall. The focal point of the beautiful space was the Japanese Fruticosa tree placed in the middle of the room. A single and inviting table for two sat underneath the artificial tree's wide spray.

"Here you go," she said, smiling.

"Thank you," Kathleen replied as Morgan pulled out her chair. "Excuse me, miss, but if this is a grand opening, where is everyone?"

"It's a soft launch, actually," a voice said, coming from a woman who could have been Kathleen's twin. "Welcome to Vista, big sis."

*Wow, Kathleen's sister is very pretty and they look
a lot alike. But my baby is stunning.*

Kathleen smiled as she watched her sister approach
in white pants with a matching, double-breasted jacket
and a tall chef's hat. Morgan stood back as the two
women embraced and the hostess disappeared behind
two closed doors.

"What's going on, Hannah?" Kathleen asked her sister in French. Switching languages was an automatic
reflex whenever Kathleen was around her family.

"Later. Right now, introduce me to this fine-ass
handsome man staring at us like he's seen a two-headed
naked lady," she replied.

Morgan laughed. "He understands French, Hannah.
Morgan, this is my sister Hannah Winston," Kathleen
introduced, switching back to English.

Morgan extended his hand. "Pleased to meet you,
Miss Winston."

Hannah shook his hand and said, "Call me Hannah.
We're almost family," she teased.

"Stop it, Hannah," Kathleen scolded.

"It's cool," Morgan replied, smiling at both women.
"You have a nice place here, Hannah," he said, looking
around the empty room.

"Thanks, but this is not my place. It's my friend
Mark's, but he won't get in town until tomorrow."

"Hannah is the guest chef," Kathleen announced
proudly.

"Nice."

"Where is everyone, Hannah?" Kathleen asked.

"You two are it. You have the whole place to your-
selves…except for my staff, of course, and me. Don't
worry, we'll stay out of your way. You won't see us unless you have to. You'll have plenty of privacy."

"How do you have any type of opening with just two people?" Kathleen frowned.

"Actually, the soft opening is tomorrow night. This is more like a soft…soft opening." Hannah gestured with her hands as she glanced around the empty room.

"What does that mean?" she asked, narrowing her eyes.

"That means you two are our guinea pigs to make sure we are ready for tomorrow. So let's get this drill started." Hannah waved the waiter forward. "This handsome gentleman is Carl, and he'll be your server this evening."

Kathleen sat down, and Morgan took the seat across from her. "Can I get you anything to drink?" Carl asked.

"I took the liberty of choosing a nice chardonnay to accompany the appetizers I made for you." Hannah sent Carl to the bar to collect the bottle, and when he returned he filled their glasses. Another young woman appeared with two large square plates. She placed the plates in the center of the table after Hannah had Carl remove the centerpiece.

"I prepared a baked brie with figs and walnuts. Oh, I hope you don't have a nut allergy," Hannah said to Morgan.

"No, I don't." Morgan's cell phone rang; he checked the screen and sent the caller to voice mail.

"Good, because it's divine. There're buttered Parmesan croissants, shrimp scampi dip and baked ham-and-cheese roll-ups. Try the roll-ups. They're ham, Swiss cheese and a poppy seed glaze. Everything's delicious, if I do say so myself." Hannah's whole face lit up.

Kathleen reached for a roll. "We better try one or she'll never leave us alone."

Morgan selected one and took a bite. "This is very good."

"Yes. Hannah, it's very good," Kathleen agreed.

"Great. We have a full menu, but if you trust me I can make you something fabulous," Hannah offered, smiling at both Morgan and her sister.

Morgan raised his right hand. "I'm game."

"That would be great. Thanks, sis."

"Excellent. You two enjoy and your dinner will be out shortly." Hannah exited the room.

Morgan reached for his glass of wine and raised it. "To a very interesting evening," he said, grinning.

Kathleen smiled, picked up her glass and clinked his with hers. "It's getting off to an interesting start, that's for sure."

Kathleen filled her plate with several appetizers and watched as Morgan did the same. "Your sister's pretty great and her cooking is amazing."

Kathleen wiped her mouth. "She really is…both my sisters are."

"What does your other sister do?" Morgan took a drink from his glass, and his phone rang again. He looked at the phone's screen; his smile disappeared and his face went blank.

"Anything wrong?" Kathleen took a sip of her wine. She wasn't sure if she really wanted to know the answer to that question, but she was happy she didn't have to answer his question about her other sister yet.

Morgan exhaled noisily. "I was engaged once. To a socialite named Bonnie Ford, and she's reaching out to me again."

"I see…" Kathleen's eyes dropped to her plate and her heart fell to the floor with the thought that this woman was back in his life. She set her mouth in a hard line, preventing all the emotional craziness in her head from escaping her mouth.

Morgan reached across the table and held Kathleen's hand. "Bonnie and I haven't been anything to each other in years."

"Then why is she calling you now?"

"I'm not sure. We haven't spoken yet."

"Engaged." Kathleen pulled her hand back and took another sip of her wine. *They must have had something pretty special if she still thinks it's okay to reach out to him. Maybe he still has feelings for her.*

Morgan sighed and sat back in his seat. He could almost see the wall coming back up between them, and Morgan knew he couldn't let that happen. Morgan hated talking about the circumstances behind his breakup with Bonnie but he figured if he didn't this might be his first and last date with Kathleen.

"The Ford family was part of the same social circle as mine. We met while in high school. She went to an all-girls boarding school, so we mostly saw each other on the weekends and holidays."

"So this was just a high school thing," Kathleen concluded incorrectly.

At that, her face had brightened like a light bulb, and he hated to disappoint her. *Damn. I wish I could just stop right here, but I will not start this relationship off on a lie.* "Not exactly. More wine?" He reached for the bottle.

"Yes, please."

Morgan topped off both their glasses and returned the bottle to the silver bucket where it had been resting on a bed of ice. They both took a drink before Morgan continued. "After high school, we went to the same college, and both majored in engineering. The Fords own a small refinery."

"Sounds like you two had a lot in common."

"I thought so. Even though Bonnie was pursuing her degree, all she wanted was to marry me, have kids and stay home."

"And you didn't like that." Kathleen nodded.

"Actually, that's exactly what I wanted."

Kathleen went poker-faced. "You did? Do you still feel like that?"

Here we go. I might as well ask for the check now. "If I'm honest, I love the idea of coming home and finding someone waiting for me. Not to wait on me hand and foot, if that's what you're thinking. I want a partner in every way. But—"

"But what?"

"I know this will be hard to believe but I grew up in a mostly traditional home. While my mother helped my dad out at the office a couple of days a week, for the most part, she was a stay-at-home mom when we were really young."

"Victoria Kingsley?" Doubt crossed her face.

"She wasn't always Victoria Kingsley. For a long time, she was Mrs. Alexander Kingsley and Mom. Then my dad and uncle died, and everything changed." Not knowing what Kathleen was thinking or feeling about these new revelations, their earlier conversations about his aunt and the emotions of his father's death rushing back overwhelmed him. He gripped the stem of his wineglass with more force than he realized, and it broke off in his hand, cutting him. "Ouch..."

They saw the waiter approaching, but Kathleen held up her right palm to stop his forward movement. She pushed her chair back and rose slowly and silently. Morgan sat still and closed his eyes. He was trying to bring himself back under control. Morgan felt the warmth of Kathleen's hands cupping his face. She turned his head and said, "Open your eyes, baby."

Her words and touch brought him instant relief. The emotional hurricane swirling inside him subsided. Morgan opened his eyes and stared down into the warmth of hers. She had knelt down right next to him. "What's developing between us, Kathleen, has already surpassed what I thought she and I had," he said, hoping she could see the conviction in his eyes.

Kathleen smiled, rose up and gently kissed him on the lips. "That's all I wanted to hear. Let's get your hand cleaned up. Does it hurt?"

Morgan sighed. "A little. But I want you to know everything about me. I don't ever want any lies or misunderstandings to come between us. My parents and brothers have great relationships and I want that too… with you."

Kathleen was fighting back tears at the sight of Morgan's pain and sweet declaration at the same time trying to slow her racing heart. His words wrapped around her like a warm sweater she had that once belonged to her mother. The idea that she'd been lying to him and his family about who she was and her motives for being there was making her ill.

"Carl, my man," Morgan called, waving him over. He wrapped his bleeding hand in his napkin. Kathleen stood and stepped aside.

"Yes, sir," Carl answered as he made his way over to the table.

"Do you have a first-aid kit?"

"Yes, sir, I'll get it right away."

"I think we should get you to a doctor," Kathleen suggested.

"No, it's not that bad. A couple of butterfly stitches should be fine."

Carl returned with the kit, and Hannah was on his heels. "Here you go, sir."

"What happened?" Confusion and concern were written all over Hannah's face.

"Just a small mishap. I'll pay for the glass," Morgan promised.

"Don't be ridiculous." Hannah waved off his offer. "Carl, please get this mess cleaned up."

"Yes, ma'am."

"Excuse me while I go take care of this." Morgan glanced down at his hand. "Where's the men's room?"

"This way, sir." Morgan kissed Kathleen on the cheek before following Carl to the other side of the restaurant.

Kathleen gazed after him.

"Wow, you really are into him, aren't you?" Hannah observed.

Kathleen stared down at her feet and slowly nodded. She raised her head and turned to face her sister. "Yes, I am. Too bad nothing will ever come of it." Tears began streaming down her face.

Chapter 13

Hannah took Kathleen's hand, grabbed her purse and led her to the ladies' powder room. The lounge area was large with mirrored walls; two white leather sofas and two white circle chairs sat in the middle of the room facing each other. Both women sat down on the first sofa they reached. "What are you talking about?" Hannah asked, wiping away Kathleen's tears.

"Morgan still has no idea who I am and that I've been lying to him. To his whole family."

Hannah frowned. "I don't understand."

"I just couldn't do it," Kathleen said, her voice barely above a whisper.

"Yes, you can. Let me help you."

"How?" Kathleen held her sister's gaze. "How can you help me with this? The Kingsleys thought I was there to train their staff on some new regulations. Not investigate them. I looked Morgan and his mother in the eyes and lied to them."

"Answer me this. Why do you do what you do?"

"What are you talking about?"

"Your job, why do you do it?" Hannah clarified.

"You know why. I don't want other families to go through what we did," she explained, reaching in her purse for a Kleenex.

"Right. Did you initially think you had a case against the Kingsleys? That they could be putting their employees in danger?"

Kathleen took a deep breath and released it slowly before replying, "Yes."

"If you found out that the Kingsleys had done something wrong, would you have let them get away with it?"

"No."

"I didn't think so. You were doing your job, Kathleen. Your investigation is over, right?"

"Yes."

"With a positive outcome, right?" Hannah's eyebrows rose. Unable to speak, Kathleen gave a quick nod. "So the case is closed."

"It is," Kathleen confirmed, swiping at her tears. "But I have to wrap up a few things still related to the policy writing aspect of things."

"Okay, how long will that take?"

"Not long. A week…maybe."

Hannah took her sister's hand. "So just tell him the truth then. It will be fine. I saw the way he was looking at you. He'll understand that you had a job to do. At least he won't have to worry about you being some gold digger."

Kathleen smirked. "There is that. But—"

"No buts. Just enjoy spending the weekend getting to know him better and let him get to know you too. There's more to Kathleen Winston than her net worth and job."

"Thank you, Hannah."

Hannah stood, grabbed her sister's hands and pulled

her off the sofa. "Now get up and fix your makeup. You have a handsome guy waiting for you, and I have a great meal to serve." Hannah kissed Kathleen on the cheek and left her to pull herself together.

Kathleen stood in front of the mirror and took a deep breath. She pulled her compact out of her purse and blotted her face. "Hannah was right—we're getting to know each other. This will be over soon, and I know Morgan will understand," she said to her reflection. She gave herself one last look and went back to join Morgan.

"There you are," Morgan said, standing next to the table.

"Just thought I'd freshen up. How's your hand?"

He held up his bandaged right palm. "It's fine."

"So is our table, I see." Kathleen noticed that the table had been redressed with fresh linen, new crystal glasses and dishes.

"Yes, it is. Shall we continue where we left off?" Morgan held out Kathleen's chair.

Kathleen took a seat. "Absolutely."

Morgan returned to his chair, but before he could even start their conversation, Carl returned, rolling out a two-level cart. "Your dinner is served," he announced.

"Thank you, Carl," Hannah said, coming up behind him. "Morgan, since you were such a good sport about trying my appetizers, I figured I should make you something special." Hannah raised the lids on the plates. "I hope you like your prime cut filet mignon medium rare. I know my sister certainly does."

Hannah handed them each a plate. The corners of Morgan's mouth quirked up. "I most certainly do," he replied with a broad smile.

Hannah placed a plate of asparagus and potatoes on

the table. "I'll send over a bottle of Vérité La Joie. It's an excellent red blend I hope you enjoy with your meal."

"I'm sure it will be great. Thanks, Hannah, for everything." Kathleen knew her sister was aware she wasn't just thanking her for the meal. She hated having such big lies between her and Morgan but she hoped he'd understand the circumstances.

Morgan cut into his steak and took a bite. "This is so good. It melts in your mouth."

"I'm sure it does, just like the asparagus. You should try some," Kathleen said, laughing at Morgan's plate, which was stacked with meat and potatoes, only before taking another bite of her asparagus.

Carl returned with a bottle of wine and presented it to Morgan. "Shall I open and pour?"

"Sure, and thank you," Kathleen replied as Morgan had his mouth full again. Carl offered the initial taste to Kathleen. "Excellent." Kathleen cut into her steak, tried her sister's potatoes, which she knew would be good, and smiled.

Carl filled both glasses before he returned to the kitchen. Kathleen took a sip of her wine and said, "So, a stay-at-home wife. That's what you're looking for."

Morgan held up his right index finger, swallowed his food and took a drink from his glass. "Wow, that is good. Your sister has excellent taste in wine."

"Yes, she does. She's a chef." Kathleen smiled. "Stay-at-home wife, that's what you're looking for?"

"Not necessarily. I just don't want someone who is so driven that she forgets about what's important."

"Is that what your mother did?"

"Not intentionally. After my father and uncle died, she had to step up and lead our family and run the business. It consumed her."

"That couldn't have been easy." Kathleen reached for more asparagus. "You sure you won't try any?"

"The steak and potatoes are fine."

Kathleen smiled and shook her head at the look on his face. "You don't like green vegetables?"

"Not one that looks like it's a stem of a tree," he stated, adding more potatoes to his plate.

"So is that what happened to Bonnie? She became too consumed with her career? Changed the plan on you or something?"

"Not exactly." Morgan finished off his wine and picked up the bottle. "Would you like some more?"

"Sure. And if you don't want to talk about it, that's fine." Kathleen was a pro at dodging uncomfortable questions. She'd certainly had enough practice after her mother's death and whenever she was at any social function with her family.

Morgan refilled their glasses. "No, it's fine. I want you to know me."

Kathleen felt good about his statement and willingness to open up to her, but bad because she wasn't doing the same. She told herself that Morgan would understand why she held back on him and he'd soon know everything about her as well.

"While in college Bonnie embraced her privileged life."

"What does that mean?"

"She joined what we used to call league clubs. Clubs geared to trust fund babies who liked to believe they were doing good works for others, but in reality, all they did was write checks. Nothing real was ever for anyone but themselves. It was all just for show. Bonnie insisted that we follow members of our social circle to charity events that meant nothing."

"Like what?"

"Teas, fashion shows, and we even went to the Kentucky Derby. Although that was pretty cool."

Kathleen smiled and wished she could tell him that her family went to the Derby every year: one of the perks of her wealth. Attending the race was one of the many things her mother enjoyed and one of the last they'd done together. "Because of the horses, right?"

"Right."

"So she started changing?" Kathleen concluded as she continued to eat.

Morgan held Kathleen's gaze. "Yes, her wealth became everything to her. So much so that she was no longer my Bonnie."

His Bonnie. The words stung, even though she was part of his past. "Is that why things ended?" Kathleen reached for her wineglass.

"No. Things ended because I found out that she was not only cheating on me, but she'd only agreed to marry me to ensure her family would be able to do business with my mother, which is ridiculous. Victoria Kingsley only does business with people she wants to, regardless of the relationship."

"What?" Kathleen coughed, having nearly choked on her wine.

"Are you okay?" His face twisted with concern.

"Yes, I'm fine," she assured, reaching for her water glass.

Morgan waited for Kathleen to stop coughing before he continued his story. "She'd met someone more into her, and she wanted to end things with me, but her father told her she couldn't. For the sake of the family's business and for her to be able to maintain her lifestyle, Bonnie had to marry me in order for their family to be set financially. He even told her that she could keep her old boyfriend as her lover if necessary."

Kathleen's eyes widened, and her mouth fell open. Morgan threw his head back and laughed so hard he nearly fell out of his chair.

"Oh my goodness. How did you find out about all this?"

"Bonnie told me."

"She did?"

"If nothing else, Bonnie was honest." Kathleen's heart sank at his words. "For the most part. She didn't tell me about the affair until after it started, but at least she told me herself. Bonnie even told me about her father's suggestion. She thought we should go along with it. She even went so far as to assure me that I could take a lover too."

"Wow…"

"But we'd have to abstain from those relationships when we decided to start a family. Only not right away. She was thinking five or six years from the time we married."

Kathleen's nose crinkled. "She had it all planned out."

"That she did. That was the end of things between us. That experience left a bad taste in my mouth for relationships." Morgan reached for Kathleen's hand. "Until now."

Kathleen bit her bottom lip and smiled. "Thank goodness."

"What about you?"

"I told you. I haven't dated anyone since college. I've gone out with groups of friends and coworkers to celebrate the end of a…a training session," she stuttered.

Morgan tilted his head slightly to the right and his

forehead creased. "You celebrate the end of training sessions? Those must be some difficult students you had to deal with every day. Hopefully, that will not be the case when you leave us."

"Not at all. I can honestly say that you, your company and your whole team have been a pleasant surprise."

"Even after our bumpy start?" he teased.

Kathleen laughed. "Even after that."

Morgan leaned forward, brought Kathleen's hand to his mouth and kissed her palm, sending a warm feeling throughout her body and straight south. Kathleen squirmed in her chair, trying to ease the sensation between her thighs. Kathleen held his passion-filled eyes, and without thinking, she said, "Dance with me."

Without responding, Morgan held her gaze, pulled out his phone and slid his hand across the screen. After several seconds the perfect slow song began to play. Morgan rose from his seat, came around the table and offered Kathleen his hand. Kathleen exhaled slowly, trying to calm herself. She'd never been one for slow dancing, but in that moment she found herself needing to be close to him. Kathleen placed her right hand in his, hoping he didn't notice the slight tremor. Morgan pulled Kathleen into his arms, and she instantly felt a warmth and connection unlike anything else she'd ever felt before.

Morgan felt the tremor that Kathleen tried to hide subside the moment he placed his arms around her waist. Kathleen wrapped her left hand around his neck and her right around his waist. They swayed to the sweet sound of Anita Baker's "You Bring Me Joy." Morgan felt his body respond in a way it shouldn't in a public place, but he didn't care. He looked down into Kathleen's beautiful eyes and saw his own desires reflected back at him. She raised her chin, and Morgan lowered his head and gently kissed her on the lips.

Kathleen pressed her body into Morgan and moaned into his mouth. The sound ignited a passion inside Morgan that he'd never experienced. Morgan's sex was hard as steel, and he shifted his hips in a way that ensured Kathleen could feel what she had done to him. Cupping Kathleen's face, he devoured her mouth. They kissed each other as if this would be their only opportunity, and they were both determined to make it last. When their lungs demanded air, Morgan slid his lips from Kathleen's mouth to her cheek, jaw and finally to her neck.

"Yes," Kathleen whispered, running her hand slowly across his behind.

"Damn, baby," he whispered in her ear. They were so engulfed in their passion that they didn't hear Hannah enter the room until she called out, "Excuse me."

Morgan froze and returned to his full height as Kathleen buried her face in his chest. "It's okay, baby, but I'm going to need you to stand in front of me," he whispered.

Kathleen looked up at him and uttered, "Why?"

Morgan discreetly pushed his hips against her so she could feel why for herself. Kathleen giggled and replied, "Yes, of course."

"I think it's time for the check," he said.

Kathleen smiled up at him and replied, "It most certainly is."

Chapter 14

Kathleen turned and stood in front of an expressionless Morgan. "Hannah…"

"I apologize for the interruption, but I figured you'd be taking your dessert to go," Hannah explained, giving her sister a knowing look.

"Thank you. That…that would be great. I mean, that's great," Kathleen nervously replied. She couldn't believe how out of control she'd been with Morgan in such a public venue, in spite of the privacy her sister had promised. Morgan ran both hands down the sides of her arms. She figured it was his way of calming her down.

Hannah handed Kathleen a rectangular white box with a red ribbon wrapped around it. "There are three small Bundt cakes inside. One red velvet, one chocolate mousse and one lemon." She looked up at Morgan. "Lemon's Kathleen's favorite, so you should keep it safe. I'd hate for anything to happen to it. The consequences of such a thing could be quite surprising."

"I'll keep that in mind," Morgan replied.

Kathleen knew the message Hannah was sending, and by the way Morgan responded and held on to her, she figured her threat came through loud and clear. Hannah was the baby of the bunch, but she was such a powerful force that no one messed with her.

"Can you have someone bring us the check?" Morgan requested.

Hannah shook her head. "Tonight's on me."

"I can't let you do that," Morgan insisted, pulling out his wallet and handing Hannah a black credit card. "And please, include a generous tip for yourself and everyone working tonight too."

Hannah glanced at her sister before accepting the card. Kathleen tried to keep her face expressionless and response discreet. She gave a quick nod, knowing that if she didn't Hannah would put up a fight and potentially let something slip about their identities.

"I'll be right back."

Kathleen turned and faced Morgan. "That was very kind of you."

"Don't be silly. I'd never stick your sister with such a bill, even though she was the chef. This whole night had to cost a pretty penny."

Kathleen was sure it did, and he had no idea that they could cover whatever the cost a million times over. Hannah returned with his card and receipt for Morgan to sign. He put his card away, didn't even look at the receipt and simply signed it. Morgan handed it back to Hannah and said, "Thanks again for everything. It was really great meeting you."

"It was great meeting you too." Hannah hugged her sister and walked them to the door. "Enjoy the rest of your evening. It's starting to rain, so drive carefully."

"We will. Love you, sis."

"Love you too. Stay safe." Hannah gave Kathleen a cheesy smile.

Kathleen knew precisely what her sister was refer-ring to. She was just hoping her face didn't reflect how warm other parts of her body were. Kathleen stepped out from under the umbrella the valet held for her and into the waiting vehicle. Morgan walked around the front of the car, tipped the valet and got behind wheel. They flirted and teased each other and kissed at every red light they hit.

Before Kathleen knew it, they were back at her house, sitting on the sofa on her third floor watching the rain. They opened the bottle of wine Morgan brought Kathleen earlier and shared the delicious, decadent des-serts her sister made them while discussing the latest antics of the president. "Those were really good." Mor-gan placed his fork on the plate.

"Hannah's an amazing chef." Kathleen took a sip from her glass and held it to her lips.

"You're pretty amazing yourself." Morgan checked his Piaget Polo watch and said, "It's getting late. I should go."

Kathleen wasn't sure where she found the courage, but she placed her glass on the table, climbed onto Mor-gan's lap and kissed him passionately on the lips, leav-ing no doubt about her intentions. Kathleen slid her lips across his again before she whispered, "Or you could stay." Her heart was racing, and she felt lightheaded. It wasn't the wine either. It was all Morgan. Kathleen had never been so bold when it came to men, and she didn't care if it made her look bad. All she wanted was for Morgan to say yes.

Morgan cupped Kathleen's face with his right hand and ran his thumb across her lips. He stared up into her dilated pupils and asked, "Are you sure that's what you want?"

Kathleen licked her lips. "I've recently realized that I've never really been sure of anything until now. I want you."

Morgan released a breath he didn't realize he'd been holding. He reached behind Kathleen and freed her hair from its bindings, the silky strands falling across his hands as he gazed into her desire-filled eyes. He knew her need was a mere reflection of his own.

"Where is your bedroom?"

Kathleen stood, took his hand in hers and said, "Follow me."

Morgan let Kathleen lead him downstairs to the second floor and into her dimly lit bedroom. The room wasn't what he expected. He recognized the expensive contemporary works of art that graced her bedroom walls. They were as unique in style as their owner. The king-size bed with its floor-to-ceiling wooden headboard was clearly the room's focal point. The balcony off the bedroom offered a stunning view of the city's skyline and was a nice secondary player to the room.

"Excuse the mess." Morgan knew that Kathleen was a little nervous, especially since there wasn't one thing out of place, and he found her anxiousness endearing.

"Everything's fine, baby," he reassured her, running the back of his hand down the side of her face. "We don't have to do this tonight if you're not ready," he offered, in spite of the fact that his body was screaming for relief.

"We most certainly do."

"I just don't want you to have any regrets in the morning," he admitted.

"I won't. I just hope you don't," Kathleen said, dropping her eyes.

Morgan frowned. He raised her chin, forcing her to look at him. "Why would you say that?"

"I told you. I've only been with two men, and I can count on one hand how many encounters there were."

"I know what I'm about to say is a bit chauvinistic, but you have no idea how much that pleases me. I know my number's a bit higher."

"A bit?" Her brows came to attention.

"I'm healthy, and I have protection. I've never wanted anyone as much as I want you and I'll swear that on anything."

Kathleen slid her hands around his neck, rose up on her toes and kissed him. Morgan deepened the contact, and when Kathleen gripped his shoulders and pressed her hips against his erection, he nearly exploded. Morgan murmured, "Turn around." She did as she was told.

Morgan swept her hair aside and slowly unzipped her dress. As the zipper descended and her skin was exposed, Morgan leaned down and kissed it. Kathleen's dress landed on the floor, offering him a beautiful view of her smooth, soft back and a perfectly rounded rear end in a pair of red lace panties. Morgan assumed Kathleen wasn't wearing a bra. He soon saw how both wrong and right he was.

Kathleen turned to face Morgan, and he was right she wasn't wearing a bra. Instead, he was gifted with the sight of perfectly full breasts wearing a pair of nipple pasties, designed to keep them from making inappropriate appearances. It was a battle they were losing. Morgan's insides were raging like a volcano ready to explode. He had never seen anything more beautiful. "Damn…"

"I assume you like what you see?" she asked timidly as she began to unbutton his shirt.

"You know I do." His voice was husky.

Kathleen pushed the shirt off his shoulders, and it joined her dress on the floor. She unbuckled his belt, lowered his zipper and slipped her hand inside. "Oh… my…goodness," she stammered. Kathleen wrapped her hand around his erection, and Morgan closed his eyes. The softness of her touch, the warmth of her hand and the motions she began making created a fog in his mind, and he struggled to stay upright.

"Baby, I think…you should…stop," he stuttered.

"Why?" she questioned in a soft voice while her thumb focused on his tip.

Morgan took a quick breath and grabbed her wrist. He tried to remove her hand, only she didn't release him. "Because if you don't, you're going to reduce me to a fifteen-year-old boy again."

Kathleen giggled and pulled out her hand. "We wouldn't want that, now, would we?"

"No, we wouldn't." Morgan scooped her up into his arms and carried Kathleen the short distance to the bed.

"Keep the shoes on," he ordered in an authoritative tone as he laid her down.

Kathleen smiled up at him like a Cheshire cat. "Anything you say."

"You remember that." Morgan quickly divested himself of all his clothes and shoes and Kathleen of her lace panties.

Morgan stood naked before Kathleen, standing between her legs admiring the stunning creature laid out before him. Only for him, and he had every intention of keeping it that way. Morgan knelt down and began kissing and licking his way up her body. The closer he got to Kathleen's core, the more she squirmed. Morgan gripped her thighs with both hands, hovered over her and looked into Kathleen's eyes. "I'm going to make you mine."

"Please…"

Morgan lowered his head and kissed her sex. He used his lips, tongue and teeth to devour Kathleen. Her moans of pleasure, her scent and the taste egged him on. Morgan didn't let up until he felt Kathleen's hands burrow in his hair; her body began to buck and she screamed his name. He rose up and captured her lips, offering Kathleen a taste of her exquisite delicacy.

"Hmm…"

"Delicious, isn't it?"

"Yes," she said in a low voice between breaths.

Morgan tried to move away from her, but Kathleen wrapped her arms around his neck and legs around his waist and began to swivel her hips. "Don't move!"

He knew she could feel his shaft at her entrance. It was as if the lower half of his body had taken on a life of its own. "Baby, I have to go get the condoms out of my pocket."

"No, you don't." Her head turned, and he followed her line of sight. "Gift bag."

"What about it?"

"Get it." She dropped her arms but kept her legs around him like a vise grip. Morgan knew he could break her hold but the fact that she didn't want him to and the desperate way he wanted her had his heart beating fast and relenting to her will.

Morgan reached for the bag. He removed the tissue paper, looked inside and burst into laughter. "There's, like, thirty condoms in here."

"I know, all sizes and styles too. My sister Hannah

and her friend got them for me in case things developed between us. I'd say they have." Kathleen thrust her hips forward, allowing his tip to slip inside her. "Yes," she moaned.

Morgan felt her wetness and immediately pulled back. Her unfamiliarity with this level of desire clearly had Kathleen feeling reckless. He would know because he felt it too, but one of them had to retain some sense of sanity.

"Wait, baby." Morgan emptied the bag on the bed and picked out the appropriate one for him. He rose up off Kathleen, gently breaking her hold, opened the condom package and rolled the fine level of protection on as he watched Kathleen's hands play with her breasts. When Kathleen started to remove the pasties, he uttered, "Stop. Allow me."

Morgan kissed and sucked each breast, leaving her nipples for last. After leaving his mark on the inside of each breast, something he hadn't done in years, he slowly removed each covering as if he was opening a fragile gift. Morgan tossed them aside and held Kathleen's gaze. He could see the tears forming in her eyes. Morgan's sex was throbbing at her entrance, but he knew he needed a few more seconds of sanity to get the words that had to be said past his lips.

"You are mine," Morgan declared. Kathleen nodded as she wrapped her legs around him again, raising her hips up to him. "Exclusively. I won't share you."

"Neither will I," she replied.

"You won't have to. I'm yours." Morgan thrust his hips forward, burying himself deep in her warm wetness. Her walls engulfed him like a tight shirt, and he heard her take a quick breath. He looked down at her and held still, allowing her body to adjust to his size. "Are you okay, baby?"

"Yes. You're just…big." Morgan tried to pull back, only Kathleen tightened her hold. "No. I'm already adjusting."

Morgan knew just how to help that process along. He took her nipples in his mouth and sucked, licked and pulled, fighting every male instinct in him not to immediately take what was now his. Morgan needed Kathleen to have that first sweet release before they went on a journey that would have them reaching ecstasy together. He held still and consumed her breasts, neck and lips as Kathleen started slowly rolling her hips beneath him. Her movements increased, and Morgan's thrusts supported her efforts. When Kathleen exploded and dropped her trembling legs, Morgan's control snapped.

He rose up off her, took Kathleen by the ankles and introduced the heels of her designer shoes to the ceiling. Morgan set a marathon pace that allowed them to savor every moment in each position he introduced her to. The more Morgan showed Kathleen, the more she told him she wanted to try. Morgan released something inside them both that each knew only the other could satisfy.

After reaching the pinnacle of satisfaction, they fell asleep in each other's arms, listening to the sound of the rain and their heartbeats. Morgan knew he would never let Kathleen go and that made him sleep easy.

Chapter 15

Kathleen woke to the smell of freshly brewed coffee which told her that the fancy coffee maker that Hannah insisted she get was doing its job. Kathleen was naked and lying across Morgan's body; he was still sound asleep. They'd made love several times throughout the night and again in the early hours of the morning. She kissed him gently on his bare chest and eased off him, then slowly walked to the bathroom; her satisfied but sore body reminded her how badly she needed to get back in the gym.

She stood in front of the mirror and barely recognized herself. Yes, she looked the same, except for a few passion bites Morgan had left all over her body. They were strategically placed so that they could be admired by only the two of them. She didn't mind because the sensation of the act of receiving them had been such a turn-on. Morgan told her it was his way of reminding her that she was his. He even encouraged her to give him a few, which she had. Kathleen figured out the difference; what she saw was happiness, real happiness. It was written all over her face. The spark in her eyes, her rosy cheeks and the wide smile that wouldn't go away said it all. She was in love, and nothing else mattered. Well, almost nothing else. Kathleen knew she had to tell Morgan the truth about everything. She just had to find the right moment.

Kathleen quickly freshened up and decided to forgo her shower. She knew how much more fun it would be if she waited for Morgan. She giggled at the thought, and she reached for her robe, wrapping her body in it. Kathleen walked down the stairs, passed through her living and dining rooms to get to the kitchen where she found her sister Hannah pouring herself a cup of coffee.

"What are you doing here, Hannah?" Kathleen glanced over her shoulder to ensure that they were alone.

"I thought we'd ride together," she stated as she poured sugar into her black coffee.

Kathleen gave her sister the once over. She wore blue jeans, a white T-shirt with a blue jean button-down covering it and running shoes. *Oh crap, I forgot.* "The Ward project."

"Yes. Was your date so good that you forgot all about our Houston Third Ward service project? We're painting and doing whatever else they need us to do today?" Hannah took a seat at the island and took a sip from her cup.

"It was, and I did." Kathleen nervously tightened her robe.

"No worries, we have plenty of time. I'll make you a breakfast burrito while you change. You can give me all the details on the way over." Hannah hopped off the chair and walked over to the refrigerator.

"Oh…okay," she stuttered, not moving. Kathleen ran a number of excuses through her mind she could use to put off her sister at least a few more hours. The idea of leaving Morgan right now was the last thing she wanted.

"How late did he stay last night?"

"Pretty late," she said, knowing her face was probably in full blush mode.

Hannah peeped around the refrigerator door. "You want cheese, right? I always get confused if it's you or Kennedy who doesn't like cheese on their burritos."

"Yes, I like cheese but—"

"Good. Why are you so flushed?" Hannah returned her focus to the contents of Kathleen's refrigerator.

Before Kathleen could respond to her sister a pair of large arms engulfed her body. His natural smell, along with her vanilla body wash, was an intoxicating scent. Her body automatically leaned back into him and she closed her eyes. Kathleen felt at home in Morgan's arms. She hated they didn't have the chance to share the shower.

Morgan kissed her cheek and softly said, "Good morning," in her ear.

Hannah closed the refrigerator door, and Kathleen's eyes popped open.

"I see." Hannah gave a lopsided grin.

"Good morning, Hannah," Morgan greeted her, keeping his hold on Kathleen.

"Well, good morning," Hannah replied, placing the contents in her hands on the island. "I'm guessing everyone had a good night." Her eyes were bouncing between Morgan and her sister, who had suddenly gone mute.

"We did, and thanks again for the wonderful meal last night," Morgan said.

"You're welcome. I'm about to make another one.

I hope you like breakfast burritos. With or without cheese?"

"With cheese, of course. Can I help?" he offered.

"You sure can."

Morgan kissed Kathleen's hair, walked around and stood next to Hannah. Kathleen stood, still unable to speak, and watched them making breakfast together. She couldn't get over how handsome Morgan looked wearing last night's clothes. Kathleen watched in awe at how easily Morgan got along with her sister. Hannah was an easy person to like, but their wealth and her celebrity status made her guarded around others, something she and her sister shared, only Kathleen had kept people at a distance for the sake of her career. At least that was what she told herself.

"Don't just stand there. Get the plates ready and pour us some glasses of OJ," Hannah commanded.

"Sure." Kathleen went to her cabinets and pulled down three plates and three glasses and set them on the island. Kathleen could feel Morgan's eyes on her as she walked over to the coffeepot, selected two mugs that hung from the wall and turned to face her guest. The smile that Morgan gifted her was breathtaking; she'd never seen him so relaxed and she found it very attractive. Kathleen held up a cup and said, "Want some?"

Morgan's smile widened. "I most certainly do."

"Coffee... I mean coffee," she nervously clarified, trying not to blush. It was a feat she failed miserably at, by the smirk her sister sent her way. All the Winston women tended to turn crimson whenever they got embarrassed, nervous or really angry.

"I take mine with cream and—" he held up two fingers "—two sugars."

Kathleen poured coffee in both cups, pulled the

cream out of the refrigerator and added the appropriate amount to both cups, added the sugar and handed him his coffee.

"Thanks, baby." He held her gaze, and Kathleen smiled. She loved the term of endearment he'd begun to use.

"I'm good. Thanks for asking," Hannah said sarcastically.

"I was going to top off your cup too, sis."

"Let's eat before our masterpiece gets cold," Hannah stated, handing Kathleen her plate.

Kathleen looked down at the perfectly rolled stuffed burrito and took a whiff. "This smells divine, Hannah." She always admired the many masterfully compiled dishes her sister created in her kitchen.

"It was a team effort," she said.

"Not really," he countered. "But thanks for sharing the credit."

They sat at the island and ate. Morgan questioned Hannah about her training as a chef while Kathleen kept quiet. She loved how easily he seemed to fit in, which made her happy and sad all at the same time. Happy because she could see a real future with Morgan and sad because her lies could ruin it all.

"Baby, you okay?" Morgan asked as he rubbed her back.

"Yes, I'm fine. Why do you ask?" Kathleen frowned.

"Because you've barely touched even half your food."

"I'm full. I don't usually eat such a heavy breakfast. It's delicious, though."

Having finished off his burrito, Morgan reached for Kathleen's plate. "We can't let this excellent food go to waste." Both women laughed. "So what are you two lovely ladies doing today?"

Kathleen half shrugged. "Nothing—"

"Actually, we're helping to rehab the community center not too far from here," Hannah interjected.

Morgan wiped his mouth with his napkin. "Oh yeah, what kind of rehab?"

"Painting, refurbishing some of the wood furniture, tile work in the bathroom, stuff like that. Did my sister tell you—"

"Hannah—"

"That she refurbished all the floors in her house?"

"She most certainly did." Morgan gave Kathleen a proud smile before leaning over and kissing her on the cheek. Kathleen released an audible breath, which didn't go unnoticed by her sister. Hannah's brows snapped together, and she mouthed the words, "What's wrong?"

Kathleen set her face straight. "Could you use another set of hands?" Morgan asked.

"Really?" Kathleen's whole face lit up, in spite of the fact that her lies were making her sick. She knew she had to tell him the truth as soon as possible, but the idea of spending more time with Morgan made her very happy.

"Sure. I love doing service projects. Plus, I get to spend more time with my girl." He ran the back of his hand down the side of her face.

Kathleen loved the idea of them working together on such a worthy cause, but she wasn't sure this particular project was the right one. "That would be great but—"

"Yes, it would. We need all the help we can get if we're going to meet next weekend's grand opening."

Kathleen was trying to think of a counterargument, but she couldn't think clearly with the way Morgan was looking at her, and his constant touches clouded her mind. "You don't have anything to wear and didn't you mention something about going to see your brother and nephew?"

"Nephew?" Hannah asked.

"Yes, I have two. My older brother and his wife just had their first baby a few weeks ago. And my brother KJ—"

"The NBA player? I guess former NBA player is a little more accurate of a description," Hannah interrupted.

Morgan nodded. "Yes. He and his wife have a four-year-old son and will have another baby soon."

"That's great, Morgan." Kathleen could see the pride in his eyes.

"Yes, it is. I just saw Alexander's son, but I haven't gotten to spend much time with Colby since KJ had them out on the road with him. Now that he's retired, I'll get to see a lot more of him. He's a cool little dude too. I can't wait for you to meet him, Kathleen," Morgan said.

"So you want kids? Do you have any?" Hannah asked, back in protective sister mode.

"Hannah," Kathleen chastised, giving her sister the evil eye.

The corners of Morgan's mouth rose. "It's fine." He reached for Kathleen's hand and intertwined their fingers. "Yes, I want kids…with the right woman." Morgan squeezed Kathleen's hand but kept his eyes on Hannah. "And no, I don't have any children yet."

"Good answers," Hannah replied as she started cleaning the kitchen.

Kathleen rolled her eyes skyward. "Sorry about my nosy sister's question."

"No worries. Your sister's just looking out for you."

"What about your plans?" Kathleen asked, handing her and Morgan's plates to Hannah.

"I'll just call KJ and tell him we'll see them to-morrow."

Kathleen's heart stopped. Yes, he'd said he wanted her to meet his nephew, but she didn't think he meant now. As if she read Kathleen's mind, Hannah turned and faced her sister. "We?"

"Yes, of course, unless you have other plans."

Kathleen stared at Morgan in disbelief. He was open-ing up to her in ways she never expected. Everyone knew how fiercely private the Kingsleys were and yet Morgan wanted to share his life with her while she kept hiding hers.

"No, she has no plans," Hannah stated for a shell-shocked Kathleen.

One of the many daggers Hannah was shooting Kathleen with her eyes hit its target and snapped her out of it. "I have no plans."

"Good, you had me worried there for a second."

Kathleen frowned. "Worried?"

"I thought maybe my mother had you scared. Look, I know my family's wealth and power can be over-whelming and the media can be intrusive. I try to fly under the radar, so hopefully, they'll leave us alone. I promise I'll keep you safe."

Kathleen fought back tears, and her mouth was sud-denly very dry. She knew about trying to hide from her family's wealth and influence. Kathleen reached for her orange juice and finished it off. "Yes, your mother is scary, but it's fine. I can handle it."

"That's my girl," he said, bringing their hands to his mouth and kissing the backs of them. "I keep clothes at KJ's apartment. I'll go change and be back in less than an hour."

"You keep clothes at your brother's house?" Hannah

questioned, wiping down the island, having loaded the dishwasher. Kathleen was curious about that herself.

"Yes, at his old apartment downtown. He and his family are staying in his wife's old house until their new one is built. They've been having so many construction issues—maybe he should hire Kathleen," he teased.

"Maybe he should," Hannah said, smiling.

"Don't be ridiculous." Kathleen's eyes narrowed at her sister. "I'll walk you out."

Morgan held Kathleen's hand as they walked to the front door. As soon as they'd cleared Hannah's view, Morgan pulled Kathleen into his arms and kissed her in a way that left no doubt about how much he wanted her. Kathleen knew she was falling for him and only hoped he felt the same way about her. When he finally let them both breathe again, he asked, "Should I bring an overnight bag back?"

He looked like he didn't know the answer to that question. Kathleen rose up on her bare feet, wrapped her arms around his neck, gently kissed him on the lips and whispered, "Yes."

Chapter 16

Morgan made his way to his brother's apartment feeling like he was on top of the world. He'd finally met someone he believed was perfect for him. Someone he felt he could trust. He knew she didn't come from a wealthy background like his own, but hers must be somewhat privileged. Her artwork, furnishings and home told him that much; even if she'd bought her house at auction, it would have cost her a pretty penny. None of that mattered to him. He'd seen firsthand how his world could affect people like Bonnie and her family when they weren't used to it, and Morgan was determined not to let such differences come between him and Kathleen. He wanted a future with her.

After parking in front of his brother's apartment building, Morgan spent a few minutes speaking to the security guard before making his way up to KJ's penthouse. When he opened the door he was met with a big smile and a loud shout of "Uncle Morgan."

Morgan knelt down and scooped up Colby, swinging him in the air. "Hey, Colby. How's my favorite four-year-old nephew?"

Colby frowned. "I'm not four anymore. I'm five." He held up his right hand to support his assertion.

"That's right. You did have a birthday. Sorry I was out of town and missed it. You did get my gift, right?"

"Yep, you want to see it?" He squirmed until Morgan placed him on his feet and he went running to the back of the apartment.

KJ came out of the kitchen, saying, "Slow down, son."

"Okay, Daddy." Colby slowed his pace.

"Good morning," KJ greeted him.

"Morning." The two men bumped fists. "What you two doing here? Is Mia here too?"

"No, she's getting a haircut or trim…something, hell I never know. Want some breakfast?" KJ asked, leading Morgan into the kitchen.

"No, thanks."

"You sure?" He held up a kids-targeted cereal box. "Breakfast of champions."

"I'm sure," Morgan said, laughing at the funny expression on his brother's face. He found himself wondering if one day he'd be making that same offer to someone, only it would be his and Kathleen's kid's cereal. That thought didn't scare him in the least bit either.

Colby ran back into the kitchen but slowed down when he saw his dad's face. He held a fire truck nearly as big as he was. "Here it is, Uncle Morgan."

"Let me see that. Man, this is cooler than it looked online."

"It makes noise too," Colby informed him.

"Yes, it does," his brother agreed, giving Morgan the evil eye. "Remind me to return the favor one day."

"You might be able to sooner than you think."

KJ went expressionless. "Colby, you done eating?"

"Yes, Daddy."

"Then take your truck back to your room and watch cartoons while I talk to your uncle."

"Okay."

"Here you go, little man." Morgan handed Colby back his truck. "See you later."

"See you later, Uncle Morgan."

Both men stood and watched Colby leave the room. Morgan looked at his brother and smiled. "That's one great kid you got there."

"I know, and I'm blessed to be able to claim him as my own," KJ admitted.

"How's he doing…healthwise?"

"He's great. We're extra cautious when his asthma acts up. It can cause so many other issues in kids with Down syndrome, but we've been really lucky," he explained.

"That's good."

KJ leveled a look at Morgan, and he knew the turn the conversation was about to take. "Now, what's this about me being able to return the favor? Want to tell me something, brother?"

Morgan shook his head. "No, not yet."

"Sit," KJ ordered, taking a seat at the island. "Now you got me curious."

Morgan sat and rubbed his hands together. "I met someone."

"Seriously?"

"Seriously, and man, she's something special." Morgan's heart started beating so fast he felt like the sound might drown out the words he was trying to express. "I've never met anyone like her before. If you take Mom's strength, Aunt Elizabeth's kind heart and the beauty of all my sisters-in-law, you'll have my Kathleen."

KJ's eyebrows stood at attention. "Your Kathleen."

"She's family-oriented, knows the oil and gas business and she doesn't take my crap." Morgan was so engrossed in his description he nearly missed his brother's comment.

"She really must be something special. How long have you known this woman and where did you meet her?"

"I only met her a few weeks ago. She's the trainer that OSHA sent to update our systems and training program based on some new regulations that just went into effect," Morgan explained.

"Don't you think that's fast?"

"You know me—"

"I do, which is why I am asking. You don't get involved. At least not long-term," KJ stated with a worried look on his face.

"Neither did you until you met Mia," he reminded KJ.

"True. Even then I fought it."

Morgan nodded in agreement. "So did I but I couldn't seem to help myself."

"I know the feeling. Congratulations, man." KJ offered his hand, and the two men shook. "So when do I get to meet her?"

"I was going to bring her with me when I came to your house tomorrow, if that's cool."

"Tomorrow? What happened to tonight?"

"We have this other thing we need to do and I'm not sure when we'll be done or what shape we'll be in by this evening. Will tomorrow work?" he asked, hoping for a positive response.

"Of course. There will be plenty of BBQ."

"Great."

"Yep, you got it bad."

Morgan laughed. "I know."

"So what brings you to town anyway? Don't say it's just to see us," KJ questioned.

"I took Kathleen to dinner last night."

"Last night. Well, I know you didn't spend the night here, so I assume you two…"

"I should go change," he said, ignoring his brother's conclusion. "Kathleen and I are meeting her sister at a community center for a service project."

Morgan figured KJ got the hint that he didn't want to go there with him when he changed topics and said, "So she has a sister."

"Yes, and she's an amazing chef."

"A chef?"

"Yes, she has some popular show," Morgan offered, his forehead creased as he tried to remember the name of her show.

"That's cool. What's her name?"

"Hannah Winston. You know it?"

"No, but Mia might. She's really into cooking networks," KJ explained.

"She has two other siblings too. Her brother's in finance, I think, and her older sister is an executive. At least I think that's what she told me. I honestly don't remember what she said," he admitted. "I do know they all seem to do well for themselves."

"Well, I'm happy for you, man." Colby's laughter rang throughout the house.

"Me too, for you, as well. What time tomorrow?"

KJ shrugged. "How's one?"

"Sounds good to me. I'm going to change. I can't keep my lady waiting." It was a declaration that Morgan was beginning to enjoy making.

Kathleen sat on one of the chaise longues in her closet with her body and hair wrapped in towels. She looked up at her frustrated sister, and she knew she couldn't keep this conversation at bay any longer.

Hannah stood in front of Kathleen with her arms folded across her chest. "Now that you've had your shower, do you want to tell me what's going on? Why are you in such a frenzy about Morgan coming to help us today? The man is obviously crazy about you. He couldn't seem to keep his hands off you."

Her sister's words broke through the dam Kathleen built to hold back her tears; the truth of Hannah's statement was too much to bear. Kathleen burst into tears. Hannah sat down next to her sister and put her arms around Kathleen. "What's wrong?"

"I'm falling in…love with… Morgan," she said between sniffles as she tried to catch her breath.

"Oh, sweetie, that's okay. It's pretty clear to me he's fallen for you too."

"I know…" A fresh set of tears fell.

Hannah released her sister, left the dressing room, returning quickly with a box of tissues in hand. "Here you go." Kathleen took a tissue and blew her nose. She wiped her tears and took several deep breaths trying to calm herself. "Talk to me, Kat."

Kathleen offered her sister a weak smile at her childhood nickname. "I still haven't told Morgan the truth about everything."

"What?"

"I know, I should have told him." Kathleen dropped her face in the palms of her hands.

"Yes, you should have."

"I—"

"Kathleen, you had sex with the man without clearing the air about everything." Kathleen nodded, keeping her hands on her face. Hannah put her arm around her shoulders. "It's okay."

Kathleen dropped her hands. "No, it's not."

"No, it's not, and I shouldn't have encouraged you. I forgot how emotionally inexperienced you are and I don't want you to get hurt," Hannah stated. "But you *are* going to tell him, right?"

"Yes, of course. I was waiting for the assignment to end, but now, I'm going to tell Morgan as soon as my boss officially closes the case."

"I thought you did that already?"

Kathleen saw the confusion in her sister's eyes. "I did, but I don't have the final say."

"Well, when will that be?"

"Hopefully Monday, and I'll tell Morgan everything as soon as I know."

"Why does that even matter? I mean, you said they were innocent. Why not just tell Morgan now?"

"Because my deception was about business that I let turn personal—"

"But only after you'd determined that they were already innocent."

Kathleen shook her head. She stood and walked over to the dresser. "That doesn't matter. I still deceived him…them, and I put my reputation and job in jeopardy."

"How did you do that?"

"I got involved with the target of an investigation,

Hannah. That crosses all types of ethical boundaries," she explained, throwing her hands up in disgust.

Hannah heaved a sigh. "So what are you going to do?"

"I'm going to get this case closed, come clean to my boss and tell the Kingsleys the truth. I'm hoping when I explain things and give them the good news about the outcome of the investigation they might find a way to forgive me," she rationalized.

"And if they don't?"

"I don't know," Kathleen admitted.

"Well, if Morgan cares for you like I think he does, he'll find a way to move past it. I'm sure of it," Hannah stated with confidence.

"It's not just that."

Hannah stare fixed. "What else is there?"

"He doesn't realize we come from an equally wealthy background."

Hannah gave a nonchalant wave. "Oh that, that's nothing."

"It's something to him."

"I can't believe he hasn't figured it out." Hannah ignored her buzzing phone. "All he has to do is search the internet for you or me, for that matter."

Kathleen exhaled. "Thankfully he's not into social media."

"All right, but what does all this have to do with the service project?"

The look of confusion had returned to her sister's face.

"Dad supplied all the materials for this job."

"So…" Hannah frowned.

"So? Don't you think he'll find it odd that we're

doing a service project with a bunch of Winston materials lying around the place?"

"First off, our donation was in the form of money and workforce. They could purchase the materials from many different places, and our name isn't on any of them." Hannah started walking around her sister's closet, checking out her wardrobe. "You've been out of the business too long."

"So have you," Kathleen countered.

"Yeah, but I know what's going on and that we don't make the materials we use," she snapped back.

"You're right. Sorry, sis. I guess my paranoia is getting to me."

"It's fine. Look, I think you're concerned over nothing, but I'll head over now and make sure there's nothing out there that says Winston Construction or that there's no one's around to blow your cover, okay?"

"Thank you."

"No problem." Hannah hugged her sister. "Keep the faith, and I'll let myself out. See you soon."

"Hannah's right. Just keep the faith. You can do that because Morgan's worth it. What we have is worth all the risk," Kathleen told herself.

Chapter 17

Kathleen moved in front of her full-body mirror. She loosened her robe and looked down at the evidence of her and Morgan's passion last night and that morning, and all of his words came rushing back into her mind. Kathleen took a deep breath and released it quickly. "Everything is going be fine. As soon as you get dressed," she said, pointing to her reflection.

She opened her dresser drawer, selected a black lace bra and underwear set and slipped them on. She pulled out a pair of blue jeans, a green V-neck shirt and a blue jean jacket. Kathleen put on a pair of blue running shoes, lightly made up her face and pulled her hair up into a high ponytail. She was gathering up the towels when her doorbell rang. Kathleen tossed everything into her hamper, picked up her phone and purse and went downstairs to open the door.

"Hi." Kathleen was taken aback at the sight of Morgan in black jeans, a tan short-sleeve shirt, black leather jacket and black oxfords; she loved his more casual look. He was holding a brown leather bag and her heart raced because she knew what that meant. Kathleen stepped aside to let Morgan inside. As soon as he crossed the threshold, he dropped the bag, pulled Kathleen into his arms and captured her lips in a mind-blowing kiss. "Oh, wow."

Morgan leaned his forehead against hers. "I missed you," he admitted. His voice sounded weak.

"I missed you too. I'm guessing those are a few of your things."

"They are. Should I take the bag upstairs?"

"Later. We have to get to the Ward Community Center. You look great, by the way," she complimented.

"So do you, like always. I love the jeans, although they'll make keeping my focus that much more difficult." Morgan opened the door. "After you, my lady."

As they made their way to the community center, Kathleen shared its eighty-year history in Houston's Third Ward with him. She explained how the residents came together and contacted several companies to get support in bringing their community center back to its former glory. She left out the fact that her family's company had been their largest benefactor.

When they finally arrived at the center, Kathleen quickly scanned the area for any Winston Construction signs that might've been posted. Kathleen breathed a sigh of relief when she saw none. They exited the vehicle and headed inside.

"There you are," the center's director said as she approached Kathleen.

"Good morning, Mrs. Benson." Kathleen kissed the slimly built gray-haired older woman wearing a long flowered dress with a white apron wrapped around her waist.

"Good morning." She brought the glasses that hung around her neck to her eyes and checked the clock on the wall. "I guess it's still morning…barely. Now, who is this handsome gentleman?"

"Mrs. Benson, this is a friend of mine, Morgan Kingsley." Kathleen turned and looked up at him. "Morgan, this is Mrs. Benson. She's an old family friend, and she spearheaded the campaign to get this center updated. As a way to thank her for all her hard work, the community voted to make her the center's director."

"That's what I get for opening my big mouth," she teased, extending her hand.

Morgan gave her hand a gentle shake. "Pleased to meet you."

"Morgan came to help us out today. I'm sure you can find something for him to do." Kathleen looked around the center's entrance and all the boxes, furniture and sporting equipment that littered the foyer and every hallway leading from it.

"Are you good with your hands?" Mrs. Benson asked.

"I most certainly am," he replied, briefly cutting his eyes to Kathleen.

Kathleen felt warm all over, and she only hoped she wasn't as scarlet as Mrs. Benson's nail polish. "Morgan's family owns an oil and gas company, so he's always working with his hands," she quickly explained.

"Good. Head down that hall," she pointed to the left of where they stood. "Knock on the last door to your right and ask for Danny. He has a couple of walls that need a coat of paint."

Morgan reached for Kathleen's hand. "I guess I'll see you later."

Kathleen squeezed his hand and smiled. "I'll come by and check on you in a little while." She watched as he walked away and her heart immediately started to ache. Kathleen was starting to feel like she was losing something important. *Get it together, girl. Everything's going to be fine.*

"Hello…" Mrs. Benson snapped her fingers in front Kathleen's face.

"Yes, ma'am," Kathleen replied, snapping out of her trance.

"Someone's smitten, I see. I say that young man is more than just a friend."

Kathleen didn't want to be disrespectful to Mrs. Benson, but she didn't want to discuss her personal life with her either. *Deflect.* "Where do you need me today?"

"The library, of course. We still have to fill all those beautiful bookshelves you refurbished for us. I still can't get over your father's generosity. First, he donates all the money we need to restore and upgrade this place, and then he sends us thousands of books to fill our library shelves, so we're ready the day we open. Or should I say the Irene Winston Memorial Library."

Kathleen smiled. She loved the idea of the library being named after her mother.

Kathleen's mother had been an avid reader, especially during the last year of her life. Irene had an eclectic taste when it came to books. She loved everything except romance novels. Kathleen's mother once told her that the reason she didn't read about other people's romances was because she was living one of her very own. Kathleen now knew exactly what her mother meant.

"It was his pleasure. My mom was a big fan of reading."

"I know she was, sweetie." Mrs. Benson ran her right hand down Kathleen's arm as if she was trying to warm her up. "We better get to work."

"I'm on it. Just one more thing."

"What's that?" Mrs. Benson placed her right hand on her hip.

"Morgan doesn't know anything about my family's wealth and I'd like to keep it that way."

"He won't hear about it from me," she promised.

Kathleen sighed. "Thank you. I'll get to work."

Morgan stood in the doorway of the room he'd been directed to. He saw an older brown-skinned man with a shaved head wearing a blue shirt and a pair of overalls and work boots painting a wall. "Excuse me, sir, are you Danny?"

"Yes, how can I help you?"

"Hi, I'm Morgan Kingsley." He offered his hand, walking into the room. "I'm here to volunteer, and Mrs. Benson sent me to you."

"Did she now? I can't shake your hand but welcome. Do you know anything about painting?"

"Yes, sir, I sure do."

"Good. As you can see all four walls have been primed and are ready to be painted."

"Yes, sir, I can see that. Where would you like for me to start?"

"You can start by losing that fancy jacket of yours and rolling up your sleeves."

Morgan smirked. "Yes, sir." He removed his jacket and laid it across the chair near the door. He held out his arms. "Short sleeves, which wall do you want me to do first?"

"You're a young and virile-looking man, so you get the back wall," Danny said, laughing. "Everything you need is in the corner."

Morgan poured paint in a tray, selected a roller and got to work. After toiling in silence for nearly an hour,

Danny asked, "So what brings you here? I didn't see Kingsley Oil and Gas on the list of donors."

"You know who I am?" Morgan studied the older man.

"Of course, I spent twenty years as a longshoreman. I know all the companies in the gulf," he declared proudly.

"I didn't know anything about this project," he stated as he continued to work.

"I see. I thought maybe you were here anonymously."

"No, I came with a friend," Morgan said, silencing his ringing phone.

"Who, if I may ask?" Danny stilled his brush and looked over at Morgan.

"Kathleen Winston," he said proudly as his heart skipped a beat when he just mentioned her name.

"Kathleen's a good girl from a great family." Danny returned to his work.

"Yes, she is. Kathleen's something special."

"Did I hear my name?" Kathleen asked, walking into the room.

Danny put his brush down and hugged Kathleen. "Yes, you did, beautiful one. How are you?"

"I'm good. How have you been?" She gave Danny a quick kiss on the cheek.

"Fit as a fiddle."

Kathleen laughed. "I see you put this one to work." She gestured with her head toward Morgan.

"I sure did. Excuse me a minute." Danny left the room to answer his buzzing phone.

"Speaking of work, shouldn't you be doing some?" Morgan teased.

"As a matter of fact, I should. I just wanted to make sure you were handling your assignment okay."

Morgan laid down his roller, closed the distance between them in less than three strides and wrapped his arms around Kathleen's waist. "You sure that's all you wanted?" He gave her a wicked grin before leaning forward, kissing Kathleen passionately on the lips.

Sooner than either one of them wanted, Morgan ended their kiss, a move Kathleen clearly rejected by tightening her grip on his waist and back. Morgan took her hands and gently removed them from around him. His body was coming alive in a way he knew was inappropriate.

"Baby, we're in public," he whispered in her ear.

"It doesn't seem to matter where we are. I can't think when you kiss me like that," Kathleen admitted.

"Is that a bad thing?"

"I'm not sure. Bad things can happen when you don't think."

Morgan brushed a loose strand of hair from Kathleen's face. "Not if you're following your heart," he countered.

"Is that what we're doing...following our hearts?"

Morgan knew he was entering foreign territory and it unnerved him. He was determined not to let fear or his past ruin something that could be amazing between him and Kathleen. He stared into Kathleen's eyes, ran the tips of his fingers across her lips and said, "I am, and I hope you are too."

Kathleen rose up on her toes and snaked her arms around his neck. "I am too," she whispered gently, kissing him on the corner of his mouth and running her tongue across his lips before kissing him again.

Morgan was so lost in the gentleness of her touch, her kiss, that he hadn't heard Danny return. "You two keep that up, we'll never get this room finished, and I'd like to get home before the storm hits," he said, returning to his wall and paintbrush.

Kathleen turned in Morgan's arms and faced Danny. "There's a storm coming?" Morgan heard her tone rise an octave.

"Yep, and it is supposed to hit sometime tonight," Danny stated nonchalantly.

"You can't be afraid of a little rain. You certainly weren't afraid last night," he whispered in her ear.

Kathleen nudged him with her elbow and looked over her shoulder. "No, I'm not afraid of a little rain. It's the rapidly rising water that scares the hell out of me."

"It will be fine. My brother's house sits off the road, anyway."

"About that." She turned to face him, pulling out of his hold. "Can we step in the hall for a second?"

"Sure. I'll be right back, Danny." Morgan followed Kathleen out the door.

"What's going on?"

"Don't be disappointed, but I don't want to go with you to your brother's house tomorrow."

"Why, because of the rain?" His forehead creased.

"No. I just think things are moving a little fast. Maybe we should slow things down a little."

Morgan's frown deepened as he folded his arms and cocked his head to the side "Do you? You just said—"

Kathleen bit her bottom lip and dropped her shoulders. "What I meant...*mean*, is that we need to figure out what this thing is between us before we share it with others. It should be our secret. At least for a little while."

"You mean *you* need to figure out what this thing is, because I'm crystal clear." His annoyance was on full display. He couldn't believe this was happening...again.

Morgan ignored the goo-goo eyes two young volunteers sent his way as they passed them in the hall. His eyes bored into Kathleen.

"I just think it's a little soon to go public and start sharing it with more people."

"People…"

"Yes. Our whole family, friends…people we work with," she explained.

"Don't you think it's a little late? The secret is out."

"No, it's not. Just because *some* people know or maybe suspect we went out doesn't mean we're in a relationship. It's no one's business," Kathleen declared emphatically.

"It seems you don't know what this is, do you?" Morgan felt like he'd just been hit in the gut. He wanted a committed relationship with Kathleen and all that entailed, but it seemed she wasn't quite there yet. Morgan might not have been in a relationship for a while, certainly not one like he wanted with Kathleen, but he knew doubt in or about relationships never worked.

"I just think—"

"Don't worry about it. Take all the time you need." They stood silently staring at each other for several moments. "I should get back in there."

"Okay. I'll get a ride home from Hannah so you don't have to change your original plan and can go over to your brother's house tonight from here. I'd hate for you to get caught in the storm."

"If that's what you want." He dropped his arms. Morgan was choking on his hurt and anger. Hurt because he thought they were falling for each other and now he realized it was only just him, and anger because he'd sworn he'd never let this happen to him again. But he let his guard down, had given his heart to Kathleen, and she'd shoved it back in his face after stomping on it.

"I'll see you later?" She reached for his hand.

"Later." He gave her hand a small shake and walked away.

Kathleen stood and watched Morgan walk back into the room to join Danny. She'd felt sick throughout that conversation. Kathleen knew exactly how she felt about Morgan and she'd love nothing more than to shout it to the world. Unfortunately, she couldn't do that until she told him the truth about everything. The idea of expanding her lie to more of his family was something she couldn't handle and wasn't willing to do. The hurt she saw in his eyes pained her heart. The only thing she held on to was the idea that this would be over soon and everyone would know they were together and in love. She just had to stay strong and hope Morgan would too.

Chapter 18

Kathleen returned to the library and buried herself in work. That was what she always did whenever things in her life got hard. It didn't matter if it was her day job or hobby distracting her; she gave whatever it was her undivided attention. Working hard was her safe haven. She only stopped long enough to eat the contents of the lunchbox her sister had provided; something that was supposed to be a simple ham-and-cheese sandwich with a bag of chips ended up being a gourmet creation on a croissant with sweet potato fries. Hannah had even added a small version of one of the Bundt cakes she'd made her and Morgan the night before, bringing tears to her eyes.

After Kathleen placed the last set of books on the shelf, she stretched her arms out at her sides and rolled her neck. The hours of sitting, reaching and bending had taken their toll on her body. Much like Morgan had the night before. Kathleen had managed to push her concerns over Morgan out of her mind long enough to get her project done, and she was quite pleased with the outcome.

She looked around the room. "What do you think, Mom?" Kathleen felt a sense of warmth come over her and while she was pretty certain it was her imagination, she said, "Yeah, I like it too."

"You ready to go?" Kathleen turned to find Hannah standing in the doorway holding her bag in one hand and checking her cell phone in the other.

"What?"

"Morgan told me to be sure that I got you home safe."

"He did?" Kathleen frowned. She had hoped Morgan would have insisted on taking her home himself. It would have given her time to explain herself better.

"Yep. I thought you two would be inseparable all weekend, based on what I saw this morning," Hannah replied, keeping her eyes on her phone.

"That was before I put my foot in my mouth," she murmured.

"You two meeting up later?"

Hannah hadn't heard a word Kathleen had said, which was fine with her. "I'm sure."

"Where did he go?"

"He's hanging out with his younger brother," she explained. Kathleen decided to let her sister believe everything was fine between her and Morgan. She didn't want Hannah worrying about her. This was her problem to fix.

"Boys' night out," Hannah concluded. "You two starting to do couple stuff already? That's cool, just make sure he doesn't have too many boys' nights out. But by the look of things, I'm sure that won't be a problem."

"Yeah, keep them at a minimum. Got it."

"Well, let's go, I want to take off before the weather changes. You know how much I hate flying in the rain."

"Flying? Where are you going?" Kathleen picked up her purse, pulled out her phone and checked for a message from Morgan. She hid her disappointment at having found none as they left the center, only stopping long enough to say their goodbyes to Ms. Benson.

"I'm heading back to LA."

Kathleen frowned. "I thought you had the restaurant opening tonight."

"Yeah, about that, I kind of stretched the truth a bit."

"What do you mean you *stretched* the truth a bit?"

Hannah shrugged. "Last night was the soft…soft opening but real soft opening isn't for another couple weeks."

Kathleen's face contorted. "Do I even want to know what you had to do to make last night happen?"

"Nope." Hannah winked at her sister.

Kathleen gave her head a slow shake. "Thank you."

"Trust me, it was my pleasure making that happen for you two." Hannah's eyebrows started to dance. "Duty calls. This visit was fun, but between the show and my social commitments, I can't take any more time off."

"You work too hard," Kathleen observed.

"Hello, pot, pleased to meet you," Hannah replied with her left eyebrow raised.

"I know… I know, just call me kettle," Kathleen admitted, and they both laughed.

Hannah dropped her sister off at home, and after a tearful goodbye, Kathleen let herself in the house, nearly tripping over Morgan's bag. Kathleen closed and locked the door, dropped her keys and purse on the entry table and made her way to the kitchen where she pulled out a bottle of Stella Rosa Rosso from the wine refrigerator. She selected a glass from the cabinet, poured enough to ease her frayed nerves and finished off the contents, barely letting the taste settle on her tongue. After eating such a big lunch, she wasn't hungry. Kathleen topped off her glass, grabbed the bottle and headed back to the foyer.

Holding the glass and bottle in one hand, she picked up her purse and stared down at Morgan's bag. "Stop tempting me. I'm not calling him," she declared, picking it up. "I'm taking you upstairs just to get you out of the way," she explained as if she was talking to someone.

Kathleen placed her purse and the wine bottle on the dresser while she set Morgan's bag on the steamer trunk that sat at the foot of her bed. She stared at it while she took several more sips from her glass. "Stop it!" Kathleen topped off her glass, walked into her bathroom, started the water filling up her Jacuzzi tub and stripped. She lit several candles and dropped two bath beads in the water.

She finished off her drink and set the empty glass on the counter, slid into the warm water and let the tub and wine relax her. Kathleen's mind flashed back to the bath she'd shared with Morgan last night. He'd insisted on bathing her after the second time they'd made love. The way his large, masculine hands roamed her body sent sensations throughout her the likes of which she had never experienced before. Kathleen laid her head back against the tub's built-in pillow, and her hands followed the path Morgan's had. She touched her neck, breast and stomach as she closed her eyes and pictured Morgan's face. She let her legs fall open, slid both hands over the wet, soapy hairs that covered her sex, inserting the index finger of both hands inside her.

Between the rush of the water and the rapid movement of her hips, Kathleen soon brought herself to an orgasm, moaning Morgan's name. She opened her eyes and waited for her rapidly beating heart to slow its pace. As soon as she could move, Kathleen got out of the water, drained and cleaned the tub. She stepped into her shower and let the warm water and body spray finish what she'd only just started.

Clean and completely relaxed, Kathleen wrapped her hair in a towel and dried her body with another. She slipped into a robe, collected her wineglass, stood in front of the dresser and began drying her hair. Kathleen stared at Morgan's bag through the mirror, wondering what all he might have packed. Before her curiosity could get the best of her, Kathleen heard her iPad ringing. She was receiving an incoming video call.

"Well, hello, stranger," Gilbert stated, waving.

"Stranger? I talk to you every day," she reminded him, pouring the last of her wine into her glass.

"No, you send me work to do every day," Gilbert stressed, frowning. "When was the last time we actually sat down and shared some good tea?"

"I don't have time to sit around gossiping with you during the day. And neither do you, given all the work I send your way."

"I'm an excellent delegator."

Kathleen glared at Gilbert. "You're not overworking our intern, are you?"

"What do you mean by 'overwork'?" he asked, using air quotes.

"She better not quit, Gilbert," Kathleen warned him, feeling somewhat annoyed but not surprised and trying not to laugh.

"Calm down. Hard work builds character. Isn't that the BS line you always use on me when I complain about being overworked?" he reminded her.

"Yes, but she already has character," Kathleen said, laughing.

"I'll let you have that one. Hey, whose Prada bag?" His eyes widened.

Kathleen glanced over her shoulder before returning her attention to Gilbert. "It's nothing. Nothing to worry about. You aren't driving, are you?"

"Of course not. I'm in a car service heading downtown for drinks and maybe even a little dancing. You want to join me? I'm not far from your place. I can be there in no time."

"No thanks. Go have fun," Kathleen replied, brushing her hair. "I'll talk—"

"Oh no, you don't, nice try. You can either tell me right now what's going on or in twenty minutes when I'll be at your place."

"I hate you." Kathleen sighed. "CliffsNotes version." She picked up her iPad and sat on her bed where she explained just how complicated her life had gotten these past few weeks.

"Damn, girl." Gilbert shook his head. "Was he at least worth it?"

"Really? Is that all you have to say?" Kathleen lay across her bed, watching the rain hit the bedroom window. Her mind flashed back to the night before, when she had Morgan in her bed. Tears welled in her eyes and she reached for the pillow that Morgan used, gripping it as if it was a life buoy.

"You don't need me to say anything else. I'm sure you've already beat yourself up for crossing the line with the target of your investigation. And you're *really* kicking yourself for not going with Morgan to his brother's house tonight. So all there is left to ask is— was it worth it?" he reiterated.

Kathleen propped her head up with her left hand. "Yes, yes, it was."

"Then you know what you have to do," he said, raising his eyebrows.

"Refresh my memory."

"Call him and get him back there so you can enjoy the rest of your weekend. Come Monday morning, officially get the case closed and tell him the truth about everything."

"That's the plan, but I think I'll let him hang with his family. I'll see him Monday."

"Okay, if that's what you want, but before I go, open his bag and tell me what all he has in there," he said, making his eyebrows dance.

Kathleen laughed. "No, I'm not invading his privacy."

"I don't know why the hell not. He invaded all your privacy last night." Gilbert screamed in laughter.

Kathleen covered her face and mouth, laughing. "Boy, you are a mess."

"You sure you don't want to come out? I'm here, but I can be at your place in no time. It's barely nine."

"I'm sure." Kathleen was in no mood to socialize, despite having her spirits lifted. She'd made her decision and now all she had to do was wait.

"How about I run inside for a quick drink, and I'll come hang out with you after?"

"That's sweet, but I'm fine, really, I promise. Once the truth is out and I have a chance to talk to Morgan, I'm sure everything will be fine. I hope so, anyway. You just be careful."

"I will. Later." Gilbert ended the call.

Kathleen set her music to play before closing her iPad, sat up and placed it on her nightstand. She stared at Morgan's bag. "No, don't even think about it." She jumped when she heard a clap of thunder. *Chill.* Kathleen got up, grabbed her glass, walked downstairs and into her kitchen. She selected another bottle from her wine refrigerator and filled her glass. Kathleen stood in her kitchen, drinking her wine, staring down at her unpolished toes. "We need a pedicure bad," she said, wiggling her toes.

Heading back upstairs, she stood in the doorway of her bedroom, staring at Morgan's bag. *Don't do it.* "What the hell. A little peek won't hurt," she justified. Kathleen placed her glass on the dresser, stood in front of the bag and slowly unzipped it. The moment she opened the bag, the scent of Morgan's cologne filled the room. It wasn't an overpowering smell like it had spilled from its container. It was more of an aroma that wrapped around her like a warm blanket.

You've had your peek. Now close it. Kathleen's heart, body and mind were at odds. She ran her hands over the clothes at the top of the bag, savoring the feel of his black silk pajama top. Before she could stop herself, Kathleen untied her robe and let it drop to the floor. She pulled out the silk pajama top and slipped her body inside. The arms were too long and it fit her like a dress, but to Kathleen, it was perfect. The silky-smooth feel of the fabric against her skin and the combination of Morgan's natural scent mixed with his cologne made her feel safe. It was the next best thing to being in his arms.

Kathleen closed her eyes, wrapped her arms around herself and began swaying to the Teddy Pendergrass song "You're My Latest, My Greatest Inspiration." It was one of her parents' favorites. She and her siblings had watched them dance to it many times. Kathleen seriously missed both Morgan and her mother in that moment. Just as the song was coming to an end, she heard her doorbell ring, and she knew it was Gilbert. He never believed her whenever she said she was fine and he knew she was upset and sad about something. Gilbert was a great friend, but he couldn't fix everything, no matter how hard he tried.

"I'm coming, Gilbert." Kathleen picked up her glass, taking a drink from it as she went to greet her persistent friend. "I'm fine," she said, opening the door.

"That you are." Morgan's eyes roamed Kathleen's body. "Who's Gilbert?"

Kathleen's heart raced. She just knew Morgan could hear the rapid flow of her blood in her veins. Kathleen was so happy to see him she couldn't speak. The shock of his presence made her forget that she was wearing his clothes.

The corners of Morgan's mouth rose. "May I come in?" Kathleen nodded, and she took two steps backward.

Morgan had spent the last few hours brooding at his brother's apartment after canceling his plans for the evening and tomorrow; he knew he'd be terrible company. All Morgan could think about was Kathleen and how badly things had turned so quickly. He realized she might not be feeling the same way he was about her and he had to respect her request.

Intellectually, he knew that was the right thing to do. Unfortunately, his heart and body had another idea, which was what led him to her home. Morgan wasn't letting Kathleen go, even if he had to keep their relationship a secret. Kathleen was his. But first...

Chapter 19

Morgan crossed the threshold, closing and locking the door behind them. He leaned back against the door, placing his hands in his pockets so he wouldn't reach for her. Not yet, anyway. Morgan needed answers. He crossed his feet at the ankles. "Who's Gilbert, Kathleen?"

"We work together," she replied, speaking softly.

"So you're expecting a coworker…dressed like that, in my nightshirt. My favorite nightshirt, at that." Morgan was fighting to keep his emotions in check. He didn't want to jump to the wrong conclusions. Only he prayed that they would, in fact, be wrong. Morgan couldn't imagine his Kathleen doing such a thing, even if she was angry at him.

Kathleen's face reddened, and her free hand flew to her throat. She glanced down at herself. "I'm sorry. I shouldn't have…"

"It's fine. You look beautiful and sexy as hell. I just hope it's not for someone else."

"I'd never do such a thing." Kathleen lowered her

head, dropped her shoulders and said, "Morgan, you're the only man I want."

Morgan released a deep sigh that prompted Kathleen to raise her head and capture his gaze. He thought his heart would burst through his chest any second. Morgan pushed off the wall and closed in on Kathleen like an animal after his prey. He removed the glass from her hand, placed it on the nearby table and picked her up. Kathleen threw her arms around his neck, and her legs wrapped around his waist. They kissed as if their lives depended on the connection. Morgan walked them to Kathleen's bedroom where he tried to place her on the bed, but Kathleen refused to release him.

"No," she whispered between kisses.

Morgan cupped her face with both hands. "Baby, just give me two minutes, and we'll make love all night," he promised.

Kathleen dropped her arms and legs and watched as Morgan quickly undressed and rolled on a condom. She unbuttoned his nightshirt and opened it, putting her body on full display. Morgan stood, staring down into her gorgeous face. His eyes dropped to her breasts and erect nipples. He leaned forward and slid both hands slowly up her thighs. Kathleen shivered, and Morgan smiled, knowing he caused that response. Morgan hovered over Kathleen with his erection playing at her entry.

"Please," Kathleen begged with her eyes closed, raising her hips to meet his shaft.

Morgan stared into Kathleen's face, his heart pounding in his ears, as he tried to keep his caveman instincts under control. He had to get the words he'd been dying to say out. "Kathleen, look at me," he demanded. When she complied, he saw more than desire, which was all the encouragement he needed. "I'm in love with you."

Kathleen blinked twice before the first of many tears fell. "I…I love…you too," she stuttered.

Morgan lost control and his inner caveman took over. He made love to every inch of Kathleen's body. It was like all the years of love he'd stored away for the perfect woman, a woman he never expected to meet—his perfect woman—were released into Kathleen. Morgan had every intention of leaving his mark on Kathleen, body and soul, just as she'd left on his.

Morgan and Kathleen spent the rest of the night and all day Sunday making love and plans for a future they both wanted. They shared a few household chores: laundry, making food and cleaning the kitchen. They even made time to catch a few of their favorite political shows. Morgan noticed that Kathleen didn't seem too concerned about the nasty weather outside and he hoped that had everything to do with his presence. Morgan even tried to convince Kathleen to move in with him and come work for his family as a full-time trainer. However, he was willing to make the daily three-hour commute by car or hour and half by helicopter if she didn't want to leave OSHA or Houston. Morgan really didn't care what she did as long as they were together. He knew things had developed quickly, but Kathleen didn't seem to mind and even agreed to think about his every request, which was all he needed.

Monday morning arrived before Morgan knew it. Kathleen had explained that she needed to go into her Houston office for a few hours but would be at the plant as soon as possible. Waking up with Kathleen in his arms, making love, getting dressed together and having her send him off with a big kiss and a travel mug full of coffee, knowing he'd see her again soon, was a scene he was happy with and ready to replay again and again.

Morgan walked into the office to find Adrian pacing, holding a manila envelope. "Good morning." Morgan took a sip from his mug.

"You're late," Adrian snapped.

"Last time I checked, I was the boss. What's got you so riled up this morning?"

"This." Adrian handed him the envelope.

"What's that?" he questioned before taking the envelope in his hands.

"That's something you need to see for yourself."

Morgan pushed out a breath. "Fine. I'm in too good of a mood, and nothing in this envelope is going to ruin it." He placed his mug on the desk.

"Sorry, man…"

Morgan frowned as he saw the distress on his friend's face. He opened the envelope and scanned the contents. His jaw clenched. "Where did you get this?" His tone was hard and he was trying to keep his anger under control.

"It was under my door when I got in this morning along with a note."

Morgan's frown deepened. "Where's the note?"

Adrian pulled it out of his pocket and handed it to Morgan. *Your boy is being played.* "Thanks, I'll take care of it."

"You sure?"

"I'll talk to you later."

Adrian left the room, closing the door behind them.

Morgan took a seat behind the desk. He gripped the arms of his chair as he felt his rage building. He picked up the desk phone, threw it across the room and watched it hit the wall, shattering into pieces. It was exactly the way his heart felt: shattered. "Damn you, Kathleen."

Kathleen approached her office door and found Simpson with his back to her, talking to someone she couldn't see. "Good morning," she greeted him as she entered the room wearing her blue power suit. She had to have a hard conversation with her boss today, and she needed the added confidence this particular outfit provided.

"Good morning," he replied, turning his body and allowing his guest to be seen.

Kathleen froze as she met the intense glare of the woman sitting at her desk. The scowl on her face told Kathleen everything she needed to know. Victoria knew the truth. "Your timing is perfect. I was just telling Mrs. Kingsley the good news."

Kathleen shifted her focus to Simpson, but she could feel Victoria's eyes boring into her. If looks could kill, she would have been incinerated the moment she stepped into the office. "Good news?"

"Yes. I was just explaining that the investigation into her company has closed and that our top investigator had cleared Kingsley Oil and Gas of any wrongdoing personally," Simpson explained proudly.

"An investigation I knew nothing about until I received a call from one of my many helpful friends, telling me about a complaint that had been filed against my company weeks ago. I came by to discuss the situation with Mr. Simpson when he informed me that the case had already been closed. While I appreciate your findings—" she tilted her head slightly to the right "—I don't appreciate your methods."

"I apologize, Mrs. Kingsley, but we felt that was

the best way to keep the press out of it until we knew for sure there was nothing to the complaint. Kathleen was following our directives," Simpson stated, excessively blinking. It was a nervous habit he had whenever he was around powerful people he feared, and he had every right to fear Victoria Kingsley. They both did. Kathleen could see Simpson literally and figuratively sweating as he tried to appease Victoria but Kathleen knew Victoria's anger was directed more at her than the agency itself.

"Do you think I can have a moment alone with your top investigator?" Victoria pointed to Kathleen.

"Of course." Simpson happily left the two women alone.

"I love your artwork. Máximo Laura's tapestries are exquisite. I have a few of his works myself. In fact, I believe I sent someone to purchase yours for me but was told someone beat me to it. I guess now I know who that person was. Having just found out about all this, obviously, I haven't had time to look into your background. I have to ask myself how a woman working for a government agency affords such expensive artwork." Victoria gave Kathleen the evil eye. "What are you selling, positive investigative reports? Or maybe you're threatening companies with false investigations. What's your game, Miss Winston?" Victoria demanded, sitting forward in the chair.

Kathleen couldn't blame Victoria for being suspicious of her. After all, she had lied to both her and Morgan. "I'm not playing any games, Victoria." Victoria shot Kathleen a look that sent a chill down her spine. "Mrs. Kingsley, please let me explain."

Victoria intertwined her hands, rested them on the desk and gave Kathleen her undivided attention as if she was expecting to be dazzled by some tall tale. "Please…"

Kathleen took a seat in one of the guest chairs. She took a deep breath and released it slowly. "First off, I'm Kathleen Winston from New Orleans, Louisiana, and I'm one of four heirs to the Winston construction empire." Kathleen figured that was the fastest way to clear up any concern she had about her financial ability to purchase her artwork.

Victoria's brows stood at attention. "*You're* Jonathan Winston's daughter?"

"Yes, ma'am, one of them. Do you know my father?"

"Yes. We have a few friends in common. However, it's your sister Kennedy Winston that I'm most familiar with."

Kathleen nodded. That wasn't a surprise. Her family did a lot of business in Texas, and Kennedy was a formidable businesswoman. Of course Victoria knew her. "Kennedy is brilliant."

"She must be, to hold her own in such a male-dominated field like construction," Victoria said with what sounded like admiration in her voice.

"Much like you, Mrs. Kingsley."

Victoria's eyes softened a bit. "Why aren't you working in your family's business and why did you think you had to lie to my son and me?"

Kathleen's heart sank as she fought back her tears. She dropped her head and said a silent prayer for strength and Victoria's understanding. Kathleen knew she had to get through this without breaking down, but she wasn't sure she could. Now all she could do was wait for her prayer to be answered. Kathleen sighed, pushed back her shoulders and began to explain how this whole mess started.

After laying out the origin of the complaint, finding that it wasn't based on facts and Kathleen's reasons why they felt they had to deceive them, Victoria raised her right hand. "So in spite of your superior's initial objection to investigating my company you convinced them they needed to move forward."

"Yes, ma'am, I did." Kathleen knew it was the right thing then and she stood by her decision even now, although she was second-guessing her methods.

"Why?"

Instead of offering the argument she'd used to convince her bosses to move forward, Kathleen decided to share a truth she only recently realized, thanks to Victoria's son. Kathleen cupped her hands and set them in her lap. She began to explain how what had happened to her mother affected her. Her mother's death triggered a need to seek justice for her loss. The company responsible for her mother's death had long since been closed, thanks to her father.

Kathleen directed her anger at other organizations accused of doing the same or similar acts. She admitted that she had been single-mindedly focused when it came to her investigative role and it served her well professionally. "I had been right about every single company we went after until now. The moment I realized that fact, I closed the case. I'm sorry I lied to you, but I was doing my job, regardless of my driving factors."

Victoria sat expressionless. "Just doing your job?"

"Yes, ma'am." Kathleen pressed her lips together and raised her chin almost defiantly. She had laid out her case, and now she waited for the judgment.

Victoria reached for her ringing phone, read the caller's name and sent the call to voice mail. "Was part of your job getting my son to fall in love with you?"

Kathleen gasped, and her lips parted slightly.

Victoria rose from her chair, came around the desk and stood in front of Kathleen. She leaned back against the desk; her hands gripped its edge and she stared into Kathleen's eyes. "Was it your job to take a man who didn't trust his women romantically and make him not only trust you but love you? Was it your job to break my son? Because if he can't find a way to forgive you it will break him. Where exactly is *that* in your job description?"

Kathleen felt as if the air had suddenly been sucked out of the room. The idea of doing that to Morgan was breaking her heart, and she was having trouble moving what little oxygen she had through her lungs. Kathleen's tears began to flow faster than she could wipe them away. Victoria heaved a sigh and stood. She pulled Kathleen out of her chair and into her arms. Kathleen surrendered to her tears, and Victoria held her until she was all cried out.

Kathleen stepped out of Victoria's arms and said, "I'm so sorry. I would never intentionally hurt Morgan."

Victoria kissed Kathleen on the cheek. "You love my son, right?"

"Yes, very much."

"Then you know what you have to do. Morgan's going to be angry, and he'll try to push you away. Don't let him," Victoria advised, picking up her purse and phone.

"I couldn't if I wanted to."

"I get why you did what you did and I'm praying things will work out for both of you. But know this—if you ever hurt my son again, you'll have me to deal with me. Understand?"

"I do, but that won't be necessary," Kathleen promised.

"That's my girl," she said before exiting the office.

Kathleen brought herself under control, found her purse and touched up her makeup. "I'm not going to lose you, Morgan. But first things first," she vowed, reaching for her office phone. She called her boss. "Simpson, we need to talk."

Chapter 20

Morgan had managed to pull himself together because he had more pressing things to attend to than his shattering love life. The plant just received a warning that a hurricane in the gulf had shifted and was now headed in their direction. Morgan and his team had fewer than ten hours to get the plant ready and evacuate all but essential personnel. He was standing behind his desk looking over the final plans when Kathleen walked into his office and closed the door behind her. His body and heart instantly responded to the sight of her until his mind stamped them down.

"We need to talk. It's important," Kathleen said, holding her purse at her side.

Morgan dropped his pen on the desk and crossed his arms at his chest. "I don't think so." He reached into his drawer and pulled out the documents he'd received and tossed them on the desk in front of her. "Someone beat you to it. I know everything." Morgan was fighting hard to keep his anger under control. She had made a fool out of him. She had been investigating him while he was falling in love with her.

Kathleen placed her purse on the desk, picked up the pictures and press clippings and started flipping through them. "I—"

"I especially like the article about OSHA agent Kathleen Winston receiving a special award for her bravery and hard work taking on a plastics company. I *personally* like the picture of you and your sister leaving some charity event a few weeks ago with your father, construction mogul and billionaire Jonathan Winston. This must have been a rough duty for you, compared to your charity events."

"It was an event in honor of my mother," Kathleen whispered.

"Like I said, there's nothing left to talk about." He returned his attention to his plans. "You should go. The hurricane is heading in our direction. You need to get back to Houston while you can. Whatever you're investigating will just have to wait."

"My investigation is already closed. Please, baby, let me explain," Kathleen begged.

There was a knock on the door before it opened. "Excuse me, boss." Adrian entered the office holding a clipboard. "Oh...hi, Kathleen."

"Hi, Adrian," she replied in a hushed tone.

Morgan dropped his hands. "Where are we?"

"We shut down all the oil heating units and locked down the fuel storage tanks. We're in the process of storing the diesel heaters, drilling equipment and everything else on the checklist," Adrian assured him.

"Make sure the mobile gas pumping systems are drained," Kathleen advised.

"Yes, of course," Adrian replied, smiling.

A smart and beautiful liar. Bonnie 2.0. "Good. What about the staff?" Morgan asked, trying to keep his focus on Adrian, but in his peripheral vision, he could see sadness cloud Kathleen's face. While there was a part of him that wanted to hear Kathleen out, his hurt and anger wouldn't let him.

"All nonessential staff are being evacuated now." Adrian checked his ringing phone.

"And the bunker?"

"It's ready. Excuse me. I got to take this, boss." Adrian stepped out of the room.

"What's the bunker?" Kathleen asked timidly.

Morgan went poker-faced. "It's a ten-thousand-square-foot steel underground storm and bomb shelter."

"Do you really think it'll be necessary to send everyone down there?" Her forehead creased.

"It depends on the category of the storm when it hits land and whether or not we'll take a direct hit. See how that works. You ask me a direct question, I answer it." Morgan checked his watch. "You really should leave now. Get back on the road before the weather turns too bad."

Kathleen remembered Victoria's words. She loved Morgan, and there was no way she was going to walk away from him without a fight. Kathleen stood with her right hand on her hip. "I'm not going anywhere."

"Excuse me." Morgan came from around his desk, placed his hands in his pockets and stared down at Kathleen.

Kathleen could see how angry and hurt he was, but she also saw something else. She saw love and desire, and that gave her the additional courage she needed to get through the next few moments. "You heard me. I'm not leaving. I love you, and you love me. We're going to talk about this. Maybe not right now, but we will discuss everything. You say you know everything, or at least you think you do? Then you know what I'm capable of doing. Now put me to work. How can I help?"

"Fine. Stay. You can help Ms. Monica from the cafeteria. We sent most of her support staff home."

Kathleen felt hopeful when Morgan didn't dispute the fact that he loved her. "If that's where you want me." They stood staring at each other in silence. With a racing heartbeat, Kathleen conjured up a bit more courage and reached for Morgan's hand. She placed it over her heart and her hand over his heart. "I know you can feel my heart beating just as I feel yours. For as long as our hearts pump blood throughout our bodies, we will love each other. I know I have a lot to explain and account for and I will. Just know that I'm still yours and you're still mine."

Thunder roared, and Kathleen jumped. Morgan lowered his hands and snaked them around her waist. "It's okay. You're safe."

Kathleen buried her face in his chest and cried. Not out of fear but sadness for what she could have lost. Morgan held her and rubbed her back but gave Kathleen no assurances that they would be fine. He was comforting her as he would anyone else, and that just made things worse.

"Excuse me…again," Adrian announced.

Kathleen stepped out of Morgan's arms and turned her back on both men. She needed to pull herself together. She reached in her purse, pulled out a Kleenex and wiped her face.

"What's up?" Morgan asked.

"Everyone's in place. I'm headed to the watch center."

"Good, but first I need you to take Kathleen to the lounge," he ordered.

Kathleen swirled around so fast it made her dizzy. "What? I thought I was helping Ms. Monica in the cafeteria."

"You are, only the cafeteria is closed. We moved everything we need to another location. It's an enclosed area where we'll wait out the storm while we decide if it's necessary to move into the bunker," Morgan explained, his tone flat.

"Oh." Kathleen appreciated Morgan's explanation, only she wished it wasn't so professional.

"Where will you be?" Adrian asked Morgan.

"I'll make rounds and meet you at the watch center after."

"Cool. You ready, Kathleen?"

"Give me a minute please." Kathleen was talking to Adrian but looking up at Morgan. Morgan gave Adrian a quick nod and stepped out the door. Kathleen closed the distance between them, cupped his face with shaking hands, rose up on tippy toes, hoping he wouldn't push her away and kissed him gently on the lips. While Morgan didn't stop Kathleen and even returned her kiss, it wasn't quite the response she was hoping for either.

"You should go," Morgan murmured, his tone having softened.

Kathleen picked up her purse and walked to the door. She placed her hand on the knob, looked over her shoulder and said, "We're not over. We love each other too much."

Kathleen spent the next several hours reminding herself of that fact as she helped Ms. Monica prepare the lounge for what could potentially be a long stay. The large room with cocoa-colored walls and gray Berber-carpeted floors was warm and inviting. Half the room offered leather-style sofas, lounge chairs, a dining table that seated fifteen and an entertainment center with a 262-inch TV in its center. The other half of the space was being set up for sleeping; thirty cots were actively being assembled.

"Wow, this place is something else," Kathleen stated as she helped unpack boxes of prepackaged meals.

"Victoria Kingsley doesn't believe in doing anything halfway, trust me," Ms. Monica confirmed.

"I'm beginning to see that." Kathleen nodded in agreement.

"So how are things going with you and Morgan?"

"Umm…excuse me?"

"Child, please. Ray Charles and Stevie Wonder are still arguing over who saw the feelings developing between you two first."

Kathleen laughed, something she hadn't done since before she walked into her office that morning. *So much for keeping our relationship a secret.* "It's fine. I guess."

"You guess. What did you do?" Ms. Monica questioned, giving her the side-eye.

"What makes you think *I* did something wrong?"

Ms. Monica took Kathleen's empty box and slid her another one to unpack. "Because I've watched the Kingsleys' boys grow into men. I know everything about every one of them. The one thing I know for certain about Morgan is that if he decides to entrust his heart to someone else again, that's it. She's it. Once he makes that decision, that woman can count on two things." She held up two fingers. "He'll never hurt her, and he'll love her forever. If I have to guess if everything is all right between you two, it's not. So I'll ask again, what did you do?"

Kathleen knew Ms. Monica was just trying to help, but she didn't feel right about sharing so much with a virtual stranger to her. "Everything is fine…at least it will be. I hope."

Monica offered a supportive smile. "If it's meant to be, it sometimes might take a lot of work to make it so."

The corners of Kathleen's mouth rose. "I don't think that's how the saying goes."

"That's because it's not a saying. It's a fact. Now get busy. We'll have several people piling in here soon and we need to be ready."

"Yes, ma'am."

Later that afternoon, Morgan was sitting in the office watching weather reports on three different TVs, monitoring his production boards and gauges while reading production reports when Adrian jumped up and said, "That's enough. Put your shoes on and let's go to the lounge and hang out with everyone else."

"You go right ahead," Morgan replied, keeping his eyes on the center TV.

"There's a TV in the lounge, several in fact, if you must keep watching, but we both know the storm is going to miss us. We'll get hit with a lot of hard rain for several hours, but as long as our pumps hold up we'll be just fine. Just like always."

"What's your point?" Morgan asked, his annoyance taking a stand.

"My point is, you need to go find Kathleen and work this thing out."

Morgan scowled at his friend. "Aren't you the one who busted her in the first place?"

"No, that would be whoever sent me that information on her. I just thought you needed to know so you could find out what was going on. Not just end things with her. That woman loves you, and we both know she doesn't need your money. Hell, I think she may be richer than you are."

"Do you have any idea who sent it to you?"

"No. Maybe someone's upset that she picked you over them, but does it really matter? The truth is out and the question is, what are you going to do now that you know?"

Morgan tossed his pen on the table and sat back in his chair. "I don't know who I'm having a relationship with, a down-to-earth OSHA trainer or a rich OSHA investigator trying to... I don't even know. I don't know who the hell she is, man."

"She's the only woman I've ever seen you fall for in years. She's the real deal, and you know it."

Morgan heaved a big sigh. "How can I trust anything she says?"

Adrian shrugged. "Just follow your heart, man."

"I did. I asked Kathleen to move in with me before this."

Adrian's eyes got wide as saucers. "That's big for you, dude. What did she say?"

"That she'd think about it." Morgan reached for his ringing phone, half hoping it was Kathleen. Recognizing the number, he rolled his eyes skyward.

"She didn't say no. What's up?"

"I'm not sure. Bonnie Ford's been calling lately."

"Dude, don't do it," Adrian said, shaking his head.

"Don't what?"

"Go backward."

"Hell, no. I wouldn't do that to Kathleen or myself," Morgan declared.

"Good. Did Kathleen tell you she loves you?"

"Yes." Morgan's heart skipped a beat just remembering the moment.

"Do you believe her?"

"Absolutely," Morgan murmured. The emotions that he'd been keeping at bay started hovering around the edge of his sanity.

A sudden loud crash that sounded like thunder startled both men. "What the hell was that?" Adrian asked, looking around the room.

Kathleen. "What the…" Morgan stood and stared out the window before checking the board. "A transformer blew."

Adrian joined Morgan at the window. "Looks like there's a live wire dangling too."

Morgan grabbed his jacket and pulled on his rubber boots. "Call the on-site fire department, and I'll radio Jim and his team. They're in the area."

Morgan called Jim, one of their longtime production managers, as he quickly made it out of the building and into his truck. His first instinct was to go and check on Kathleen, but he knew she was in a safe place and he needed to check on his people and the situation. He drove through a treacherous downpour and flooded streets to get to the other side of the plant. The rain made a trip that would have normally only taken him five minutes take him nearly ten, during which his mind kept wandering to Kathleen. Morgan knew she'd heard what he had and was probably scared to death. Morgan's first thought was her, and that scared the hell out of him too. What if the woman he'd fallen in love with really wasn't the woman he fell in love with? He knew he couldn't go through that pain again.

When Morgan arrived on-site, everything was under control. He pulled his vehicle next to several others as well as a small fire truck. The transformer was dead, and the loose wire was being removed. "Jim, is everything all right?" Morgan called out, exiting the truck as he walked to where Jim stood in a nearby covered area with several of his men nearby.

"Yeah, that damn transformer was brand-new too. It looks like it got hit by lightning."

"You got the wire down pretty quick," Morgan said, looking up at the pole.

"We were already over here when it blew."

"Here?" Morgan pointed at the ground.

"Yep, we came to check this storage unit." He used his thumb to point at the structure they were standing in front of. "We heard it pop, and before I knew it, Bubba was dressed, up that pole and had ripped that sucker down in no time."

Morgan looked over to Bubba, who was smiling so wide Morgan could see all the teeth in his head. He walked over to the young man. "Good job. I assume you took all the safety precautions."

"Yes, sir, especially the ones Ms. Kathleen taught us."

Morgan frowned. "Kathleen?" He looked at Jim.

"Yeah, she taught the team how to control the adrenaline they were sure to feel in moments like these. It helped them stay calm so they could think. She also showed them the safest and fastest way to deal with live wires."

"I must have missed that class," he murmured to himself, scratching his beard.

"She added it to the computer-based program you already had in place," Jim explained.

"That's good," Morgan acknowledged.

"Now, David, your other fearless leader over there, jumped in the back of the truck like a cat," Jim teased, laughing.

"And Jim nearly peed his pants," David replied as he approached both men.

"Sure did," Jim admitted, laughing.

"Anyway, Ms. Kathleen told us to be aware of our surroundings. I didn't know where I was standing."

Kathleen...

David shook Morgan's hand as he put his phone away. "I have to check on the wife. She hates this weather, and she worries if she doesn't hear from me every five seconds."

Morgan knew how much David and his wife adored each other. He thought about Kathleen, and his heart sank because his love and anger were at an impasse. Morgan thanked everyone and ordered his men to the lounge and their firemen back to their station. He reminded everyone to stay vigilant but to get some much-needed rest. Morgan needed to follow his own advice, but before he could do that he needed answers. Other than Kathleen, Morgan figured he knew the one person who just might have a few.

Chapter 21

Morgan returned to the office and pulled out his cell phone. "Damn," he said as he noticed his battery was low and placed it on the quick charger. Morgan placed his iPad on its cradle as he sat, dialed the number and nervously waited for his video call to connect.

"Morgan, darling, you look stressed. Is everything all right?" Victoria asked, frowning.

"Not even a little bit."

Victoria nodded slowly and sat back in her chair. "So Kathleen told you."

"Wait, what?" Morgan sat forward and stared into the screen. "You knew?"

"That Kathleen Winston, heiress to the Winston Construction fortune, is an investigator for OSHA? Yes, I just found out."

"Why the hell didn't you tell me?" he yelled.

Victoria tilted her head to the right but remained quiet. Morgan took a deep breath and released it slowly. "My apologies, Mother. Why didn't you tell me what was going on?" he asked, his voice calmer.

"Remember when you came to me all excited and said that you were marrying Bonnie?"

"What does that—"

Victoria presented her right palm to the screen, stopping Morgan in his tracks. "Do you remember?"

"Yes, ma'am, I do."

"Do you remember what I told you?"

Morgan went blank-faced. He was in no mood for games, but he knew if he didn't go along he would never get the answers he needed. Morgan nodded. "That Bonnie was my mistake to make."

"Do you know why I said that?"

Morgan shrugged, not interested in the past but knowing he had to listen if he wanted her help. "Not really."

"Because you're just like me. I know everyone seems to think Alexander takes after me the most but in reality, it's you. If I told you what a silly little thing I thought Bonnie Ford was, you would've ignored me and married her that much faster. Fortunately, she showed her true colors before I had to intervene."

"So you let me fall for someone out to destroy our family instead?" he asked, feeling his anger rising.

"I didn't let you do anything, son, and you started falling for Kathleen before I even met her."

Morgan ran his hands down his face and shook his head. "I don't understand what you're talking about, Mother."

"I knew something special was happening between you two the day I walked in, and you were arguing over the training programs. The way she held her own with you, I knew she was something special."

"She was something special, all right…she's a liar." The words stung his throat as he spat them out and he felt like he was betraying Kathleen even thinking such a thing.

"Morgan, she was doing her job."

"And you're okay with how she went about it?" His brows snapped together.

"No, but I understand now why she did it."

"This coming from a woman who would threaten to banish us from the house if she ever caught us lying to her." Morgan threw up his hands in frustration. "You'll need to explain that one to me, Mother."

Victoria spent the next thirty minutes explaining to Morgan everything she knew about Kathleen and her situation, from the specifics of the complaint against the Kingsleys, her motivations and zeal to seek justice for those she believed were being mistreated, to the remorse she felt for being wrong after confirming that the accusations were baseless and hurting people, specifically the man she loved.

"Her mother? She did all of this because of her mother?" His tone was flat. Morgan wasn't sure how he felt in that moment.

"Yes, son, she did. You remember how that felt, don't you? How the loss of someone so important in your life makes you change how you view the world and the people around you?" Victoria's expression closed up, and she reached for a glass with red wine in it. "Do you remember, son?"

Morgan's mind flashed back to the day, several months after his father's death, when he'd written a hateful letter to his mother accusing her of loving her company and freedom more than her family because all she seemed to want to do was work. He'd lost his father, and their world was turned upside down. Victoria moved the family to a secluded ranch to ensure their safety. Only, in Morgan's young mind, this was a bitter betrayal. He thought it was his mother's way of getting them out of the way so she could focus on her business.

His father's loss, the sudden move and his mother's disappearance into work changed his idea of how wives and mothers should act. Morgan recalled vividly the night he'd left her the note. She came into his bedroom while he pretended to be asleep, kissed him on the forehead, returned the note to him and whispered, "I love and forgive you, son." They'd never spoken of the incident until now.

"Mother, I was a young, dumb kid when I wrote that note," he said, lowering his head and feeling ashamed.

"Look at me, son."

Morgan slowly raised his head and held his mother's loving gaze. "You were a child who lost his father and thought he was losing his mother too. I understood. You went from having the mother you wanted to getting the mother you needed. A mother who had to lead and protect her family and couldn't be there every day."

"Everything just changed so quickly."

"I know it did and I'm sorry that had to happen. However, it shaped you into the man you are today. A man I'm very proud of too," she said, smiling before taking another sip of her wine.

"So you think the death of Kathleen's mother did the same for her."

"Of course it did."

Morgan took a deep breath and released it slowly. "What should I do?"

"You don't need me to tell you what to do, sweetheart."

"Oh, you'll interfere in everyone else's love life but

not mine," he said, feeling happy now that the mood had lightened.

"I didn't interfere with—"

"Mother, please, stop it. Alexander and China?"

"That's been simmering for years." She gave a nonchalant wave.

"True. Okay, Mia and KJ?"

"Your brother met Mia because he had to do community service," Victoria defended herself, sipping her wine.

"Community service that you initiated with your friend the NBA commissioner," he accused, raising his left eyebrow.

"I don't know what you're talking about."

"Okay. But we all know you brought Brooke back into the company so she and Brice would stay together."

Victoria nodded her head slowly and held up her near-empty wineglass. "All I did was show a little kindness to two people who needed it. If my bringing Brooke home helped make it easy for your brother to decide something he'd already decided on, so be it." Victoria finished off her wine as if she'd just made a toast to herself.

"So why not do the same for me?"

A wide smile crawled across Victoria's face. "I have," she said, ending the call.

Morgan sat back in his chair and smiled. *Okay, Mother. I'll show a little kindness.* He picked up his cell phone and dialed the number he'd been avoiding too long. When he heard the call connect, he said, "Hello, Bonnie, it's Morgan. I'm returning your calls."

"Morgan, thank you for getting back to me."

"Is everything okay?" He could hear fear and relief in her voice.

"Well, that depends on you."

"Me?"

"Yes, first let me do something that I should've done years ago."

"What's that?" Morgan's interest was piqued.

"I want to apologize and thank you."

"For what?"

"I was terrible to you. I had no idea what real love was or what I had—"

"Bonnie, that was a lifetime ago. You don't need to—"

"Yes, I do. The love we had was special, Morgan, and I blew it over nothing…for nothing."

"Yes, it was, but it was also a young love…a kid's love. Neither one of us really understood that at the time."

"I agree, and I'm sorry we didn't have the chance to figure that out the right way and in the right amount of time too. I hope you can forgive me."

"Of course, Bonnie. Everything worked out for the best."

"Yes, it did, which leads me to my thank-you."

"Thank-you?"

"Yes, if you had gone through with my harebrained idea, who knows where we'd be right now?"

Morgan laughed. "Who knows?"

"Certainly not as happy as I am now and I only pray you have or will find someone who makes you that happy too. So thank you."

Kathleen's face, her laugh, her smell and even her recent words of love and commitment to him filled his mind. *I have.* "You're welcome. Now what else is going on? I know you didn't just call me for closure."

"You're right. I didn't call just for closure."

"What's up?"

"When we broke up, and after graduation, I went to work for my father. I dated a few of Daddy's picks before I came to my senses. A couple of years ago I met a computer whiz named Bill Wright, and we eloped."

Morgan wasn't exactly sure why he was so shocked, but he was. "I hadn't heard. Congratulations."

"Thank you. Bill's a private geek and we live a very full but low-key life now."

"As long as you're happy, that's all that matters." Morgan realized he really believed that too. Being happy with the one you loved really was all that mattered.

"I am. Well, I was."

"What's going on, Bonnie?"

"Dad's sick, Morgan. He has heart issues, and he needs to retire."

"I'm sorry to hear that."

"Me too. You know how much Dad loves working. As long as he follows the doctor's orders, he should still live a full and happy life. Me and Mom aim to make sure of it too."

Morgan smirked. "With you two in his corner, he doesn't stand a chance. He's going to be just fine."

"Here's the problem. Dad's trying to convince my husband to run the company. He doesn't want to, but Bill's like you. He'll do anything for family, especially since he lost his at such a young age."

"I'm so sorry you're having to deal with all this, but I'm not sure what any of it has to do with me."

"You know how cutthroat this business can be. Even for a small oil refinery like ours. Bill won't be able to handle it, and he'll kill himself trying. We're pregnant, and I don't want my husband to lose who he is, trying to do something he can't and doesn't even want to do in the first place," she explained.

"Why don't you run the company? It sounds like you've been doing it anyway."

"I am, but I'm having a baby, and I want to stay home. I'm done with working. I want to be a wife and mom now."

"I get that, and I'm happy for you, but again, what does—"

"I want…no, I *need*, for you to buy our company."

"What?" Morgan sat up in the chair and looked at his cell phone as if he were on a video conference call with her.

"Our company is small compared to some of the others, but it's profitable and has been for the last few years. I made sure of it. We own just about everything. We have minimal debt on the books, and we have cash in the bank."

"Your father wants to sell?"

"Not really, but none of us have much of a choice anymore."

Morgan ran the back of his left hand under his chin. "Why sell it to us?"

"Not us, you. I've done my due diligence. Every company that you've personally brought into your family's portfolio has been midsize and fetched a good price. You kept the majority of the staff—even the executive teams—and you've combined the company's names with the Kingsley brand. What was the last one? A drilling parts and service company, I believe. I heard you made the Shield brothers one hell of an offer and Shield Parts became Kingsley-Shield Parts and Service. That's a much better name, by the way. Yours is the only company my father would ever consider selling to. The Kingsleys are the only real good guys in this business."

Too bad Kathleen didn't know any of this before she pushed for her investigation to move forward. Focus, man; this isn't about Kathleen.

"Thanks, but I can't take credit for that. My cousin Kristen is the queen of branding."

Bonnie laughed. "I remember. So, will you consider it?"

Morgan sat back quietly as he tried to consider her request and what it could mean for their company but his mind kept going back to his mother's and now Bonnie's words about love and happiness, and all he wanted to do was find Kathleen.

"Send me the proposal."

"Really?" He heard pure joy in her voice, and that made him smile. Morgan was happy for her, and it was nice to know the old Bonnie was back.

"Yes, really. If everything is as you say, we'll meet your price."

"Thank you, Morgan, and whoever it is who's managed to steal your heart…your adult heart…is a very lucky woman."

Chapter 22

Kathleen sat nervously in a large leather reclining chair wrapped in a blanket, watching news reports on her iPad while listening to the rain. Everyone was standing around as if nothing was happening. It was like they were all just hanging out at a friend's house. It was after midnight, and everyone had just enjoyed a huge barbecue dinner that Ms. Monica and a few guys prepared under the back patio. A number of the staff had called it a night. Others were playing card games and watching movies. Even though Adrian and others assured her that Morgan was okay, Kathleen needed to see it for herself.

Her phone beeped. She was receiving yet more calls and texts from her family. Kathleen had told everyone that she was safe and fine, but like her, they wouldn't be satisfied until they saw it for themselves. Kathleen promised to call everyone in the morning. She was too tired, physically and mentally, to deal with anyone right now. All she wanted to do was find Morgan so they could talk. However, Kathleen knew she wouldn't make it out the door without someone stopping her.

Plus, she had no idea where he was, so she played what she would say to him over and over in her mind until she fell asleep.

It was after eight the next morning when Kathleen woke to the sound of laughter and the smell of freshly brewed coffee. She scanned the room, but there was still no sign of Morgan. "You can run, but you can't hide from me for long, Mr. Kingsley," she murmured to herself. Kathleen picked up her bag and made her way to the ladies' room, where she freshened up and put on a new set of clothes. After changing into a clean pair of jeans and a white T-shirt, she slipped her feet back into her boots and returned to the lounge.

"There you are," Adrian said, walking up to Kathleen.

"Here I am. Good morning."

"Good morning to you too. I came to tell you that we just got the all clear."

"All clear?" Kathleen's brows knitted together.

"Yes, the freeway is open, so you can go home."

Kathleen shook her head. "Did Morgan send you to tell me to go home?"

"Yes…no. I mean, he told me to tell everyone."

Kathleen turned her back to him. "Sure he did," she replied, fighting back tears.

"Look, you can ask him yourself. He just walked in."

"What?" Kathleen turned in time to see Morgan walking across the room with purpose toward her. Her heart rate increased with every step he took. He looked tired, and his beard was way past its five-o'clock expiration. The black jeans, white company T-shirt and work boots he wore screamed *sexy*.

"Good morning, Kathleen," Morgan greeted her.

"Good morning," she replied, searching his face for any signs of anger but finding none.

"That's my cue," Adrian said, walking away.

"Did Adrian tell you—"

"That it was safe for me to go home? Yes, he delivered your message." Her voice was curt.

"I'm sure you'd like to sleep in your own bed."

"Yes, I would. Care to join me?" She held his gaze.

Morgan held his hands at his sides, dropped his shoulders and exhaled noisily. "Actually I—"

"Morgan," Adrian yelled from across the room. "Morgan, you need to hear this."

They both turned toward Adrian, who had a worried look on his face. Kathleen followed Morgan over to where Adrian stood. "What's going on?"

"The hurricane missed us but Port Arthur got hit pretty bad, and Main Street is impassable. There's debris everywhere. They're opening an emergency shelter in the old meatpacking warehouse outside town."

"Let's pack up all the excess supplies we have here and get them over to the warehouse," Morgan ordered. "We can set this place up as a rest station for the first responders. We can open the kitchen here and if anyone can make it in to help out, great."

"They also need access to our heavy-duty vehicles for a few rescues. Some communities got flooded, and they don't have a way to get to the people who need help."

"Of course, whatever they need," Morgan assured him.

"Here." Adrian handed him a pink piece of paper. "The mayor wants you to give him a call."

"Thanks." Morgan turned and faced Kathleen. "You should probably go home."

Kathleen reached for his hand. "I can stay and help."

"You need to go home and get some rest. It'll be safer for you too. I don't know how long I'll be, but I'll call you as soon as I can." Morgan leaned down and gave her a quick kiss on the lips before turning to leave.

Kathleen wiped away a lone tear that fell as she watched Morgan walk away. She walked over to where she'd left her purse and pulled out her phone. "You have no idea who you're in love with. I'm not going anywhere without you, Mr. Kingsley," she said as she dialed and waited for her call to connect. Kathleen knew that there was a way she could help the town and its people who had been so wonderful to her whenever she was in town.

"Kathleen, thank God you're all right. I've been worried sick." His accent was thick and his voice full of fear.

"I'm fine, Daddy, but I need your help."

Morgan and his team spent the rest of the day and most of the evening helping the small town start to recover, from aiding with rescue operations to setting up smaller shelters. No matter how hard he tried to fight it, Morgan wanted Kathleen by his side. He knew they had a lot to work out and he certainly had a lot of questions, but Morgan loved Kathleen, and he wasn't letting her go. Morgan prayed he hadn't blown it by pushing her away, trying to keep her safe. He knew she thought the worst of him because he hadn't had time to explain. Morgan only hoped she wasn't too upset. He wanted to call Kathleen and ask her to come back but how could he after insisting that she leave?

As they drove through the town on their way back to the plant, Morgan noticed a path down Main Street had been cleared, allowing easier access from one side of town to the other. Several lights had been set up, illuminating the way. Large Dumpsters, cranes and trucks were parked on the outskirts of town. The name on the side of each vehicle—Winston Construction—caught his attention. Several black SUVs were parked in the parking lot of the largest hotel still in full operation.

"Pull over," Morgan ordered.

"What's up?"

"That's what I want to find out," Morgan stated, his curiosity aroused. He knew this had to be Kathleen's doing.

Adrian pulled into the lot, parked near the door and cut the engine. "Now what?"

"Now you go inside and have a beer at the bar."

"There's beer and food back at the plant, you know. Are you buying?"

"Don't I always?" he reminded Adrian as he exited the truck.

Both men entered the quiet lobby, waved at the familiar faces behind the desk and walked into the bar. Several men unfamiliar to him were drinking, eating and watching different sports games and the news coverage of the storm on the different TVs.

"How about that beer?" Adrian asked as he took a seat at the bar.

"Sure." Morgan sat on the stool next to Adrian and took in the environment.

"Now what?" Adrian asked, trying to get the bartender's attention. "Two long-neck Budweisers."

"Coming right up," the bartender replied.

Morgan scanned the room and noticed an older brown skinned, gray-haired gentleman wearing a gray suit sitting at a corner table alone near the bar's front window, nursing what appeared to be a glass of whiskey.

"Here you go." The bartender handed both beers.

"Thanks," they chorused.

"Can I get you anything else?"

"How about a little information?" Adrian asked.

"Information is my specialty," he replied, leaning across the bar.

"You know anything about these cats in here tonight?" Adrian asked.

"They're from out of town, and they all work for the dude in the corner," he said.

"How do you know that?" Morgan asked.

"A couple of the guys told me. They're in town to help the town recover from the storm."

"That's cool," Adrian said, reaching for the peanut bowl and pulling out several packages.

"Thanks," Morgan replied, turning to face the room.

"No problem."

"What are you looking for?" Adrian asked.

"I'll know when I see them," he replied, taking a long pull from his bottle.

"Wow, who is that?" Morgan followed his friend's line of sight."

"Wait, is that Kathleen? No…but she looks like her," Adrian said.

"Yes, she does," Morgan agreed, knowing who she had to be.

A beautiful woman wearing a red pantsuit and heels had joined the older man at the table. Before Morgan could react, Kathleen entered the bar, wearing an off-the-shoulder blue denim dress that came to just above her knee and heels that made her legs look longer than normal. Her exposed skin was like a siren's call to him. Kathleen headed for the table, offering a smile that didn't reach her eyes.

"There's Kathleen," Adrian said, pointing with his beer bottle.

"I see." Morgan stood, pulled out a hundred-dollar bill and dropped it on the bar. "You can take off if you want. I'll get a ride."

Adrian laughed. "I bet you will."

Morgan made his way over to the table. As he approached, he heard Kathleen and her guest conversing in French. Before he could introduce himself, Kathleen whipped her head around and caught sight of him. She flew out of her chair and into Morgan's arms.

"You're okay. I was so worried," Kathleen confessed.

Morgan felt whole again. He tightened his hold on Kathleen and replied, "I'm fine, baby. I'm also sorry. I should have never tried to send you away," he whispered.

Kathleen leaned back and looked up into his eyes. "I'm the one who owes you an apology and anything else that will make things right between us again," she insisted, raising her head to meet Morgan's kiss. The moment their lips touched, Morgan's body responded, and he had to force himself to remain in control.

"Kathleen Winston," a stern baritone voice called out.

"Before you two embarrass us any further, Kathleen, why don't you introduce us to the reason we had to pull our team off a multimillion-dollar job and get here so fast?" The other woman's annoyance was coming through loud and clear.

Kathleen turned in Morgan's arms. "Sorry. Daddy... Kennedy, I'd like you to meet Morgan Kingsley." Kathleen looked up at Morgan, and the look of love and happiness on her face made him weak. It was a feeling he was beginning to relish. How could he have ever doubted her?

She directed his attention toward her family. "Morgan, this is my father, Jonathan Winston, and the one with the sour look on her face is my older sister, Kennedy."

Morgan held on to Kathleen with one hand and reached to shake Kathleen's sister's and father's hands with the other. "Pleased to meet you both."

"Join us," Kathleen's father ordered, his voice stern.

Morgan recognized the tone in her father's voice and he felt Kathleen squeeze his hand. He knew she was assuring him that she was with him, no matter what, which made him relax.

"Be nice…please. He's extremely important to me," Kathleen told her family in French, taking the seat she'd abandoned that Morgan now held out for her.

After helping Kathleen into her chair, Morgan took the seat to her right. Kathleen's father tossed back his drink and waved over the waitress. "Young lady, bring me another and bring him more of whatever he's having."

"Yes, sir. Will you be having your usual, Mr. Kingsley—whiskey neat—or would you like another beer?"

"My usual, Susan, thank you," Morgan replied.

Kathleen's sister gave Morgan the once-over before saying, "Mr. Kingsley—"

"Please, call me Morgan."

"Morgan, I recently had the chance to see your mother in action. She's quite formidable," Kennedy complimented him.

Morgan's eyes cut to Kathleen. *Oh no.* Kathleen had

to make sure Morgan knew their relationship had nothing to do with her family's business. "You had the opportunity to work with Victoria. When did we get in the oil and gas business, Kennedy?" Kathleen frowned at her sister.

Kennedy matched her sister's confused look. "We aren't. I know you've been away from the business for a minute and that I'm the company's CEO, but you should know that too, Kathleen," she said before reaching for her wineglass and taking a sip. "We were at Sotheby's for an auction a few months ago. I saw her decimate the other bidders in pursuit of a stunning painting that she just had to have. It was impressive."

Morgan reached for Kathleen's hand and intertwined their fingers. "That sounds like my mother."

Kathleen breathed a sigh of relief when Morgan squeezed her hand. "I asked my father to send help for the town, and fortunately we had a crew nearby," she explained to Morgan.

"Yes, it is. I saw the equipment parked at the edge of town, not to mention all the lights illuminating the town square and Main Street." Morgan turned to Kathleen's father. "Thank you, sir."

"Here you go." The waitress returned with both men's drinks.

"Thank you and please add their drinks to my tab," Morgan instructed.

"Yes, sir." The young woman smiled and walked away.

"That wasn't necessary but thank you," Jonathan said, reaching for his glass.

"It's the least I can do."

"Actually it's not," Kennedy stated.

"Kennedy," Kathleen admonished.

"It's okay, sweetheart. What else can I do?" Morgan asked Kennedy, reaching for his drink.

"You can convince my sister to come work with her family where she belongs now that she's left OSHA."

Morgan's head snapped to Kathleen. "You quit OSHA?"

Thanks, Kennedy. "Yes. That's one of many things I needed to talk to you about."

"What is there to talk about? You're a Winston with engineering and architectural degrees going to waste. We could use you at the company we will inherit someday," Kennedy said.

Kathleen loved her sister, but right now she wanted to strangle her. Kennedy's practical side annoyed the hell out of her. "Kennedy, I have plans of my own."

"Looks like I have a lot to learn about you still," he whispered. "And I'm looking forward to it."

Kathleen giggled. "Kennedy, I—"

"Kathleen, you can't seriously be considering taking another government or low-paying job. Not that you need the money, but most places can't pay you nearly what you're worth." Kennedy's mouth was set in a hard line.

"Why is everything about money and status with you, Kennedy?" She scrutinized her sister.

"Because you're a Winston." Kennedy turned to their father. "Aren't you going to say anything?"

"Kathleen, are you in love with this young man?" their father asked in his preferred language.

She held her father's gaze as she felt Morgan's eyes on her face. Kathleen raised her chin, turned her attention away from her father to Morgan and replied in English, "Yes, Daddy. I love him very much."

Morgan released an audible sigh, brought Kathleen's

hands to his lips and kissed them. He turned to her father. "I love your daughter too, sir...very much."

"Well, that's that." Jonathan Winston turned his attention to Morgan and in English said, "When you two decide to marry, Kathleen—"

"Daddy—"

"—there will be a proper wedding. There will be no elopement. Is that understood?" he stated, ignoring Kathleen, who was shaking her head.

"Yes, sir," Morgan replied with a wide smile.

Chapter 23

"Now that that's settled, we should leave these two to do whatever. We have a plane to catch," Kennedy stated sarcastically, rising from her seat.

Jonathan Winston got to his feet and finished off his drink. "We should go."

"What... Where are you going?" Kathleen's eyes jumped between her sister and father.

"Thanks to this grand gesture of yours, we have to go smooth things out with a pretty pissed-off client," Kennedy informed her sister.

"Sorry, Daddy." Kathleen and Morgan got to their feet.

"Sir, please allow me to cover the cost for the inconvenience," Morgan offered.

Jonathan set his glass on the table. "I'm an extremely wealthy man, and I'm not talking about my ridiculously large bank accounts. I have the love of four children who mean more to me than any amount of money. Satisfying their needs and often their wants is my pleasure, regardless of the cost. Not to mention the people of this town we get to help too. I can't begin to give you a number to repay that particular pleasure."

"I can," Kennedy said, winking at Kathleen, who burst into laughter.

"Do you have to leave now? We could have dinner," Kathleen suggested, feeling overwhelmed with happiness.

"Next time. Kennedy's right. We need to go smooth Old Man Beckman's feathers. Reassure him that his building will get built on time and within budget." He extended his hand to Morgan. "Take care of my girl."

"Yes, sir." The two men shook hands.

Kathleen hugged and kissed her father and sister before walking them to their car. As he stood and watched the car pull off, Morgan leaned over and asked, "Is that invitation still open?"

Kathleen looked up, frowning, feeling perplexed. "What invitation?"

"To join you in bed."

Kathleen giggled and turned red. She pulled a key card out of her pocket and handed it to him. Kathleen hid her face in Morgan's chest as he picked her up and carried her through the lobby, down the hallway to the elevator for the short ride up three flights to her hotel room. Morgan opened her door, crossed the threshold and placed Kathleen on her feet. He backed her against the door and kissed her as if it was his last opportunity.

Kathleen gently pulled back and said, "We should talk."

"It's not necessary. I know everything," Morgan explained, then devoured Kathleen's mouth and raised her dress.

"Wait...what do you mean it's not necessary?" Kathleen asked between kisses. She could see the love and passion in Morgan's eyes, and she wanted nothing more than to satisfy the need that they both shared, but Kathleen was determined to clear the air before they went any further.

Morgan sighed, dropped his hands and took a step back. "I talked to my mother."

Kathleen's forehead creased. "Victoria talked to you. What did she say?"

Morgan took Kathleen's hand and walked over to the sofa. He sat down and pulled Kathleen onto his lap. "When I found out who you were and what you really did for OSHA, I called her. I felt she had a right to know if someone was coming for us."

Kathleen bowed her head. "I was…at first."

Morgan used the index finger of his right hand, slid it under her chin and raised her face. "I know. I also know why you felt you had to."

"I'm—"

Morgan placed two fingers over her lips. "Let me finish. Yes, I was angry when I found out the truth. Well, most of it, anyway. But in spite of my anger, I couldn't deny how much I love you. I knew there had to be more to the story. There was no way the woman… my woman…would do anything to hurt me intentionally. Not my future."

Kathleen was so overwhelmed by the sincerity in Morgan's voice and love in his eyes she could no longer hold back her tears. "I wouldn't."

"After my mother explained what happened to your mother, it all made sense."

Kathleen cupped his face. "I'm so sorry I lied to you."

"It's over." He gently kissed her on the lips.

Kathleen shifted her body and straddled him. "Yes,

it is." She rose up slightly and pulled her dress over her head and tossed it. "Now, where were we?"

Morgan smiled. "One more thing."

Kathleen swerved her hips, leaned forward and kissed him. "Just one." She pulled his shirt over his head and dropped it to the floor.

He smirked. "Why did you quit your job?"

"I was hoping you'd forgive me and make me a better offer," she explained as she unbuckled his belt and unzipped his pants.

Overwhelmed with love and need, Kathleen freed his erection, slid the fine cloth covering her sex to the side and lowered herself onto him. "Yes," she whispered, circling her hips. "Damn, no condom."

When Kathleen rose up off Morgan, he held his tip at her entrance. "We're both healthy and in love, right?"

"Yes," she moaned as his tip slipped back inside her.

"Your future's with me and you want my babies, right?" He thrust his hips upward slightly.

"Yes...oh yes," she cried out with her eyes closed.

"Then we're fine," he insisted.

Kathleen gripped Morgan's shoulders with both hands and slowly but deliberately circled her hips, engulfing his shaft. Morgan removed Kathleen's bra, caressed, kissed and sucked her breasts. They moaned their satisfaction in unison. As Kathleen's need increased, she took more control and Morgan grabbed her hips with both hands to assist in her effort. The manic pace he set had them sweating, breathing hard and then falling into sweet bliss together.

After, Morgan wrapped his arms around Kathleen and whispered, "Marry me," in her ear. She leaned back and stared into his eyes. The lump in Kathleen's throat wouldn't let the words come forward. She nodded and kissed Morgan with a great deal of passion.

After surrendering to the need for air, Morgan wiped away Kathleen's tears and asked, "How's that for a better offer?"

Finding her voice, Kathleen replied. "One I couldn't possibly refuse."

* * * * *

KIMANI
ROMANCE

COMING NEXT MONTH
Available September 18, 2018

#589 SEDUCTIVE MEMORY
Moonlight and Passion • by AlTonya Washington
A chance encounter with Paula Starker is all entrepreneur Linus Brooks needs to try to win back the sultry Philadelphia DA. And where better to romance her than on a tropical island? But before they can share a future, Linus will have to reveal his tragic secret…

#590 A LOS ANGELES PASSION
Millionaire Moguls • by Sherelle Green
Award-winning screenwriter Trey Moore agrees to look after his infant nephew for two weeks. Gorgeous Kiara Woods, owner of LA's glitziest day care, offers to help. While she's teaching Trey babysitting 101, she's falling hard for the millionaire. But can she risk revealing a painful truth that's already cost her so much?

#591 HER PERFECT PLEASURE
Miami Strong • by Lindsay Evans
Lawyer and businessman Carter Diallo solves problems for his powerful family's corporation. But when his influential powers fail him, the Diallos bring in PR wizard—and Carter's *ex-lover*—Jade Tremaine. Ten years ago, Carter left Jade emotionally devastated. Now the guy known as The Magic Man must win back Jade's trust…

#592 TEMPTING THE BILLIONAIRE
Passion Grove • by Niobia Bryant
Betrayed by his fiancée, self-made billionaire Chance Castillo plans to sue his ex for her share of their million-dollar wedding. His unexpected attraction to his new attorney takes his mind off his troubles. But Ngozi Johns *never* dates a client. Until one steamy night with the gorgeous Dominican changes *everything.*

Get 4 FREE REWARDS!

We'll send you 2 FREE Books plus 2 FREE Mystery Gifts.

THE TEXAN'S WEDDING ESCA...
CHARLENE SANDS
USA TODAY BESTSELLING AUTHOR

HIS BEST FRIEND'S SISTER
SARAH M. ANDERSON

Harlequin® Desire books feature heroes who have it all: wealth, status, incredible good looks... everything but the right woman.

FREE Value Over $20

SPECIAL EXCERPT FROM

ⓗ HARLEQUIN®
TM

*Award-winning screenwriter Trey Moore agrees to look
after his infant nephew for two weeks, and for once he's
out of his depth. Gorgeous Kiara Woods, owner of
LA's glitziest day care, offers help. While she's teaching
Trey Babysitting 101, she's falling hard for the sexy
millionaire. But can she risk revealing a painful truth
that's already cost her so much?*

*Read on for a sneak peek at
A Los Angeles Passion/
the next exciting installment in the
Millionaire Moguls continuity by Sherelle Green!*

"I had a nice time tonight," Kiara said when she reached the door.
When she didn't hear a response, she turned around to find him watching her intently.

"I had a nice time, as well." Trey took a step closer to her. "I enjoyed
getting to know you a little better." He was so close, Kiara was afraid
to breathe.

"Me, too," she whispered. His eyes dropped to her lips and stayed
there for a while. After a few moments, she forced herself to swallow
the lump in her throat.

He took another step closer, so she took another step back, only to
be met with the door. When his hand reached up to cup her face, Kiara
completely froze. *There's no way he's going to kiss me, right? We just
met each other.*

"Do you want me to stop?" he asked.

Say yes. Say yes. Say yes. "No," she said, moments before his lips
came crashing down onto hers. Her hands flew to the back of his neck
as he gently pushed her against the door. Kiara had experienced plenty

KPEXP0918

of first kisses in the past, but this was unlike any first kiss she'd ever had. Trey's lips were soft, yet demanding. Eager, yet controlled. When she parted her lips to get a better taste, his tongue briefly swooped into her mouth before he ended their kiss with a soft peck and backed away.

Kiara couldn't be sure how she looked, but she certainly felt unhinged and downright aroused.

"Come on," Trey said with a nod. "I'll walk you to your car."

How is he even functioning after that kiss? Kiara felt like she glided to the car, rather than walked. Yet Trey looked as composed as ever.

"We should get together again soon," Trey said, opening her car door. Kiara sat down in the driver's seat and looked up at Trey. He flashed her a sexy smile.

"And for the record, this was definitely a date," Trey said with a wink. "I didn't stop kissing you because I wasn't enjoying it, nor was I trying to tease you. I stopped kissing you because if I hadn't, I'd be ready to drag you into my bedroom. Which also brings me to the reason I didn't show you my bedroom. I didn't trust myself not to make a move." Trey leaned a little closer. "When we make love, I want us to know one another a little better, so I forced myself to stop kissing you tonight and it was damn hard to do so. Have a good night, Kiara."

Trey softly kissed her cheek and closed her door before she could vocalize a response. Quite frankly, she didn't think she had anything to say anyway. Her mind was still reeling and her lips were still tingling from that explosive kiss.

Kiara gave a quick wave. *I told you not to get out of the car earlier,* that voice in her head teased. She started her car and drove away from Trey's house.

"What the hell just happened?" She'd originally thought that she could avoid him or keep their relationship strictly friendly. Now she wasn't so sure. Kissing Trey had awakened desires she thought she'd long buried. Feelings she'd ignored and pushed aside.

Kiara made it to her home a few minutes later. She glanced at her house before dropping her head to the steering wheel. She was in deep and she knew it. To make matters worse, she only lived a five-minute drive from Trey's house, meaning there was no way she was getting any sleep tonight knowing a man that sexy was only a couple miles away.

Don't miss A Los Angeles Passion
*by Sherelle Green, available October 2018
wherever Harlequin® Kimani Romance™
books and ebooks are sold.*

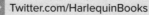